Spooky Cat Stories

C.H. Lyn

This is a work of fiction.

Cover design by Tracey Barski

Proofread by Tracey Barski

Interior art by C.H. Lyn via Canva, Tim Starkey, and Rachel Johnson

Content Warning

Hello friends. Here are a few things to have a heads up about in this story.

- Non-binary phobia
- Catcalling
- Harassment
- Mild Language
- Light Visual Horror
- Self harm in the context of a ritual
- Blood & Gore

The second installment of this story describes witch and wiccan as separate entities, one good and one bad. This is not remotely accurate and is simply used as a storytelling tool in that specific part of the series.

Contents

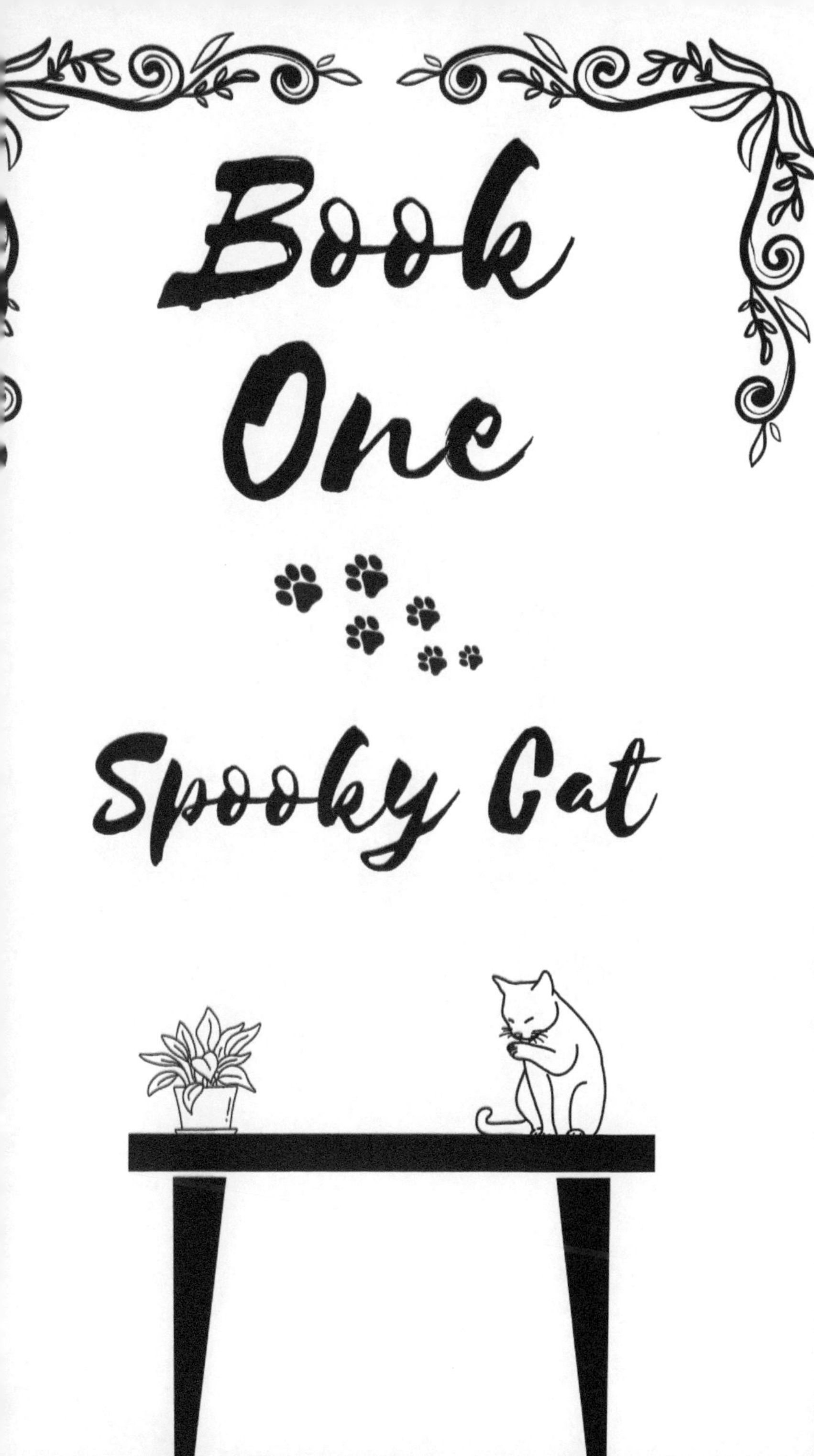
Book
One
Spooky Cat

One

My parents taught me to say "bless you" when someone sneezes, but it was Nana who told me why.

Being a kid, I laughed off her warnings. Sneezing doesn't open the door for demons, and not just because demons aren't real but because that notion is ridiculous. Or… it was.

I kept it up. Doing the polite thing long after I fell out of the habit of going to church. Little old lady on the bus? *Bless you*. Three-year-old at the grocery store? *Bless you*. Bald monk at the farmer's market? *Bless you*.

But my cat? The tiny stray who wound up in my apartment as a favor for a friend, and ended up staying because she's good at keeping a low profile when the landlord comes around?

I guess being cooped up for a year broke me of the habit.

My miniscule black cat is standing on the sill, one paw raised in the air, staring. Not at me, but at the apartment. Her gaze—no longer a moonlight yellow, but red and glinting—takes it all in. As though she's never seen it before.

The room grows cold.

"Missy..." I murmur.

Her head twitches. Flicks my direction and those red eyes look me head on.

My breath catches in my throat. My heartbeat pounds through my ears. Slowly, Missy steps from her basket, walks along the windowsill, and jumps onto the tiny kitchen table, her gaze fixed on me the whole time.

A demonic voice chills me to the bone as it says, *Missy*?

My cat's mouth doesn't move, but I know it's coming from her. From the way she stares at me, red eyes fixed on my brown ones. I hear the icy tone as though she'd spoken right next to my ear.

That's a stupid name.

A flash of irritation. I raise an eyebrow at the thing that has taken over my cat. My fingers go to the thick chords of black wrapped around my wrist. I fiddle with the gold and silver beads dangling from the leather.

"It's better than Moony." My voice is sure, stronger than it feels in my throat. "That's what they called her before she came to me."

A snort. Didn't know cats could snort.

I suppose it is better. The red gaze leaves me for a moment. Surveys its own paws. Claws—filed down a few days ago—protract and retract a few times.

I swallow.

What is this?

I walk slowly from the kitchen counter to the chair on the far side of the table from not-Missy. I sink into my wobbly seat and take a sip from my coffee, trying for nonchalant.

"What do you mean?"

This creature. Not-Missy looks up at me. *What is it?*

"It's..." I squint and cock my head to the side. "How are you in something without knowing what it is?"

I recognize the nose-twitch. It's the same one the real Missy does when I'm late with her breakfast. Or when I've used the can-opener for something besides her occasional tuna treat.

A door opened, and I went through, the icy voice hisses. *Circumstances prevented me from being overly picky.*

I nod like I understand and raise my mug to my lips. I'm proud of the lack of hand trembling as I say, "Missy is a cat."

Not-Missy blinks. They inhale. They let out a yowl that drives instinct through my cool demeanor.

I jerk back from the table and scramble to put several feet between me and the creature rolling around on the tabletop. Coffee spills from the edge of my mug. A ring forms around the pale ceramic.

No, no, no, echoes through my head.

"What..." I swallow and take another step back, my fingers moving toward a knife on the counter. At the same time, my gut churns at the thought of hurting Missy. "What are *you*?"

Not-Missy—still yowling—falls off the table. They land on their side and glare up at me from the floor. Those red eyes seem to pierce my soul.

I'm a being of shadow. Of horror and fear. Of fury and darkness. I'm a sneeze demon. Obviously.

The incredulity in their voice sends another flutter of irritation down my spine. I rest my hand on my hip. My instinctual self-preservation calms at the halt in yowling.

A snicker escapes my nose as I roll the words around in my mind. "A... sneeze demon?"

Yes, the thing snaps. *Technically I'd be called a shadow demon, but I came across via a sneeze, which makes me a sneeze demon.* Not-Missy glowers down at their paws. *I can't believe I waited five-hundred years for this chance and now I'm a cat. This is ridiculous.*

Two

"What were you expecting?"

A human. *Or at least a dog or something. I hate cats.*

Now, I'll pause the story here to say while I was lightly offended by this, I also saw an opportunity. And, wanting Missy back, I took it.

I move away from the knife, rip the last of the paper towels from the roll, and give the demon a wide berth as I cross back to the table to clean up my spill. "Is... uh. Is there any way to get you *out* of Missy so you can... try again, I guess?"

The demon squints, tilting Missy's head, and watching me with those glowing red eyes. *You'd... you'd be willing to perform an exorcism?*

"If that's what it takes, sure." I shrug, a handful of soggy, sticky paper towels in my hand. I toss them into the trashcan and rinse the bean-water off my fingers. "I don't have a lot going on today."

The eyes glint with excitement.

A shudder runs down my spine as not-Missy slinks forward. They get to the kitchen tile and leap onto the counter. The movement is familiar but hauntingly different. Like a deer walking after getting hit by a car.

Sitting with a rigid back and wide eyes, they survey me.

I resist the urge to spray them with the sink hose. Something tells me this *thing* won't react the same way Missy does when I chase her out of the kitchen.

I take a step back, finding the edge of the yellow laminate counter blocking my way. I hold up a hand. "Hang on a sec. What's to stop you from possessing me... if I get you out of my cat?"

Not-Missy's little black ears droop slightly, and they do the nose twitch again. *I'd have to promise it. And you'd have to not sneeze.*

I raise my eyebrow, the one with a studded sapphire piercing.

Not-Missy sighs. *Are there others in the area at least*?

"Dogs?"

People.

I nod. A weight pulls at my chest. "Right. Yeah. It's an apartment complex in a big city. Lots of people."

The cat nods. An unsettling sight. *I've been gone from the mortal plane for some time. Are most as impolite as you these days?*

"What?" I snap, indignant.

Not-Missy gestures with a paw. Also unsettling. *Not saying the... well, the magic words?*

I roll my eyes and heave a sigh. "You sound like my Nana." I run a hand across the cropped haircut I've been playing with. A rainbow of color hides the remaining brown. I dye it one piece at a time when I get bored. "I usually say it. But no, not everyone does. There's a drug dealer on the first floor. I doubt anyone tells him 'bless you'."

Not-Missy flinches. I make a mental note of the reaction.

"I'm just saying," I continue. "He could use a personality shift, if I'm being honest."

Hmm. The cat raises a paw to its chin. *I'd excel at selling drugs.*

I choke on my own spit and cough out a laugh. "Not quite what I meant, but sure."

Maybe not the most moral thing I've ever done, but Missy is my gal. My buddy. My cute mangy cat who curls up in my lap while I'm watching TV or sleeping.

It's been a lonely year. I want my friend back.

The apartment is quiet for a moment, save the sounds of the city outside the open window. Car horns, engines, pigeons and gulls fighting over scraps, and the constant clanging of construction a few blocks away.

Still, it feels like silence compared to not-Missy's hissing in my head.

A frown creases my brow. "What do I call you?"

The demon pauses mid paw-lick. Red eyes survey me. *I'm a demon.*

"Yes." I fold my arms across my loose-knit sweater. "That's been established. I mean, what's your name?"

They blink. Once, twice, three times as they stare at me. I suppose I've seen alarm on Missy's face before, but this isn't quite that.

I... you can call me Skia.

I nod. "Cool. Skia. I like it."

And what... what are you?

There's a question. One my parents and relatives have asked too many times for it to be confusion anymore.

I shake it off. That's not what the demon is asking. "Demi. You can call me, Demi. Now." I unfold my arms and clap my hands together. The sound reverberates through the apartment. As many plants and rugs as I have, the space is still empty enough for echoes. "How do I get you out of my cat?"

Skia jumps from the counter to the ledge a few feet away. It splits the room, bisecting the kitchen from the small couch and dining space. Standing atop, Skia eyes my drooping spider plants for a moment before looking down at the floor below.

You'll need to move these things. A tiny paw gestures to the couch and carpets. *We need a clear floor to work with. Maybe give it a mop. Skin cells will affect the ritual.*

I can't decide which part of that freaks me out. Probably the demon-cat exorcism part... but thinking about my skin cells all over the floor isn't great either.

"What else? I've got a few candles, and a couple of..." My mouth twists to the side, and I raise a shoulder in half a shrug, knowing I'm about to feel stupid. "Crystals in some of the plants."

Skia scoffs. Not in my head either, a full-on cat scoff.

I glower.

No. None of that will help. Unless your candles are fresh, eight inches tall, and white?

My teeth click with annoyance. "Nope."

Very well. We shall have to visit an apothecary.

I open my mouth, close it again, and squint up at the demon. After a moment I hesitantly ask, "When was the last time you were here, again?"

Five-hundred years ago, give or take. Why? Do humans no longer sell candles, chalk, herbs?

"We do… it's just…" I scratch my forehead. "Never mind. I'll make a list. You can wait here, and I'll pick up whatever we need. In a couple hours you'll be out, and I'll have Missy back."

Oh, I'm going with you, Demi. I'll not risk my presence on the mortal plane on you mistaking baby's breath for nightshade.

I open my mouth to object, realize I have no idea what baby's breath or nightshade look like, and give a begrudging nod. "Fine. Let me move this," I gesture to the small coffee table and the russet carpet underneath it, "and then we'll get going."

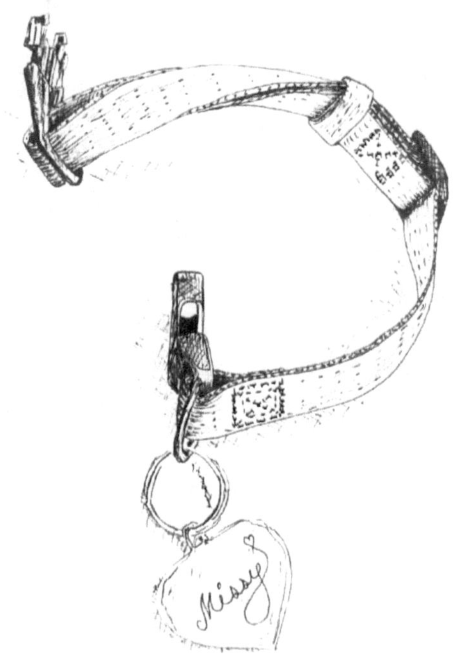
Missy

Three

I scribble Skia's list down on an old pad of DC Superhero themed sticky-notes.

No, Skia hisses, swatting at my hand. *Black chalk. Black. Get the details right.*

"Can't I use white chalk?" I ask, exasperated.

No. White chalk is for bodies. Black chalk is for rituals.

"How do you..." I squint, sigh, and shake my head. "Never mind. What else?"

I do believe that's it. Skia pads across the table.

I lean back as the demon gets too close for comfort. It's doing the thing Missy does when I try to read.

Yes. This is it. Let's go.

"Hang on." I scoot back from the table. "We can't just go out with you looking... well." I fidget with my hands. "You've got glowing red eyes, Skia."

And?

"That's not exactly... Most creatures don't have glowing red eyes. It might attract unwanted attention."

Unwanted for whom?

I hesitate here, scrambling for a reason that won't offend. "You don't want people saying—you know, the magic words. If they spot a demon running around, they might be more careful than usual."

Indeed, Skia nods, *and we wouldn't want you burned at the stake before you finish the ritual.*

"Right. Yeah, that, too."

Well then, human—

"Demi."

A cat eye roll. *Demi. What do you propose?*

I frown, click my teeth a couple times and play with the dangling pieces on my bracelet. The solution comes to me, and a flutter of fear goes through my stomach.

I look at the demon-cat. "You're not gonna like this."

Skia gestures a paw up and down Missy's chest and face. *Way ahead of you.*

I shrug. Then I go to the open closet next to my bed and rifle through a few boxes at the top.

"Here we go," I mutter, pulling a contact lens case from between a pair of fangs and pointed ear prosthetics.

What is that?

"Missy has yellow eyes... usually." I cross to the table and gesture for Skia to move closer. "I went as a vampire fairy last time they had a renaissance faire in the area."

I understand all of those words but none of the context.

I laugh, and Skia raises an eyebrow.

"Just come here and try to hold still. I have contacts to put in your eyes. They'll make it harder to tell that my cat is possessed by a demon."

Skia gives a rumbling growl that I assume is approval and plants themself right in front of me.

I unscrew the contact case, rinse off the first one, and glance at the cat that is a demon but also still a cat. "This is gonna feel weird, but hold still and it'll be done real fast."

I lean forward, one hand holding Missy's soft head while my pointer finger steadily approaches her eye. Skia flinches, jerks a bit, but I hold firm and...

"Ouch!" I wince back, the chair scraping against the ground in my hurry to move away from a bloody set of claws. Three angry lines of red mark my right forearm. Blood oozes, and I hurry to the sink to rinse out the cuts.

"What the *hell* was that?"

The cat is not pleased.

I squint and then grimace as I pump soap onto the scrapes, rubbing it in. A groan escapes my lips before I glance at the demon. "What?"

Skia glares with one yellow eye and one red one.

At least the contact went in.

Your cat is still here. Inside. And she's not pleased.

The anger fades, though the water still running across my arm stings like crazy. "Missy is like... aware?"

Somewhat. She's a cat, Demi. She's as aware as usual.

My chest constricts. "Can she... can she hear me?"

Skia heaves a sigh and plunks down onto the table, sprawling across the wood and almost knocking over the contact solution. *When she's listening, she can hear you.*

"Is she hurt though?" I shut off the water, press my shirt to my arm, and hurry forward. "Is she okay in there?"

Skia waves a lazy black paw. *She's fine. Annoyed that I'm moving around so much.* They roll onto their back and look at me upside down. *She'd rather we sit in the sun all day,* they say with a nod toward the windowsill where Missy's basket sits.

I chuckle and blink away a burning in my eyes. Then I inhale, crack my knuckles, and return to the table. "Hold still this time, okay?"

I'll try, is the sardonic response.

"Well," I grumble, "we don't want me bleeding all over the place, right?"

No, it's fine. We need fresh blood, too.

My lip curls in horror, nose scrunched up with disgust. "When were you going to mention that?"

Skia shrugs. *I assumed you'd be willing to spill a few drops for the cause.*

I grind my teeth, jam the last contact into Missy's eye, and jump back from the table before her claws can dig into me again. "Right. That's done. Let's get this over with."

Four

A few minutes later, I'm clacking down the rickety stairs with Skia close on my tail. We hurry down four flights, I pull my bike lock key from my pocket, and cross the lobby to the row of bike racks in the far corner.

My footsteps echo across the tile, followed by the soft patter of Skia.

What is this?

I halt halfway through sticking the key in the lock. I roll my eyes and scan the bike before I turn to the demon. It's... not really my aesthetic. But it was twenty bucks, has great tires, and came with the lock.

"It's my bike," I rumble out through gritted teeth.

There's a pause. I finish unlocking, pull the bike upright, and walk it to the front door.

Skia hasn't moved from their spot by the other bikes. *This is how we are getting to the apothecary?*

"Yes."

Their eyes, a little orange from the combo of yellow contacts and glowing demonic red, fix on the basket. It's white, laced through with pink, purple, and yellow flowers. The bike itself is white—or was before I rode it through the city—with a checkered purple pattern.

And where am I to sit?

I gesture to the basket. My lips twitch with the effort of not cracking a grin.

I'm. A. Demon.

I shrug. "A demon in a cat. If you want to come on the shopping trip, you've got two choices: the basket or my shoulder." I pat my left shoulder, the spot where the real Missy sits when we take trips out of the apartment.

Ugh, Skia hisses and scurries over. They hop into the basket, turn in a circle, and settle their butt down on the plastic weaving. *Fine.*

I stifle a snort, push the door open, and hold it with my hip as I roll the bike out.

The sidewalk is relatively clear. The city is large, but it's the middle of the day, and I don't live in the busiest part of downtown. A few people wander by. One smiles at the kitty in the basket and gives me a small wave.

I return it.

Skia hisses.

I swing a leg over, and plant my foot on the pedal.

Wait.

I heave a sigh. "I thought we were in a hurry?"

Do you not have protective gear for your brain?

I cock my head. "Are you concerned about me riding without a helmet?" Incredulity laces my words.

I've seen dozens of people fall from horseback and crack their skulls open. Granted, I was often responsible for startling their horse, but still.

I chuckle down at the demon. "Are you... are you worried about my safety?"

The response is less of a hiss and more of a growl before, *Not at all. If you're dead, who will exorcize me?*

A snort escapes me. I roll my eyes, tighten my grip on the handlebars, and push off. Agatha's Emporium is a dozen blocks away. I know Agatha from college. Her shop is one of the few I visit beyond the grocery store. It's got everything an introvert who hates people could ever need.

We cruise down Main Street for a few blocks, turn onto Elm, and pass the construction site. My peripheral vision catches Skia's head turn every few seconds, taking in the world rushing by.

Something clangs beyond the blue and orange wooden barrier blocking off the work, and the demon-cat nearly falls out of the basket.

"Hey." I reach out and catch their shoulder, gently popping them back into the wicker. "You all right?"

Fine. Skia glances at me. *The world is louder than it used to be.*

I respond with a nod, zipping around a car parked on the wrong side of the street, and slow as we get to a more congested part of the city. Handfuls of people wander the sidewalk. They cluster in the bike lane—idiots—and gawk at the skyscrapers around us.

"Hey!"

I ignore the voice. The person isn't familiar, but the inflection is.

"Hey!" Louder this time as a group of young men leave the bench they were crowding around and approach the edge of the sidewalk.

A low rumble bubbles from my throat as I'm forced to slow even more to avoid running into a group of middle-school-aged children sipping from to-go cups of a popular coffee chain.

There's a jeer.

I stare forward.

One of the men suggests something disgusting and calls me sweetie.

My gut churns.

In the basket, Skia glances from me to the men a few feet from us. The middle-schoolers are out of the way and I'm pedaling again, gaining speed, and leaving the assholes behind. Not in time to avoid hearing them call me a stuck-up bitch.

An inaccurate statement. Bitch and bastard are the defaults, and I'm somewhere between the two. It takes more than three IQ points to come up with a better insult, I guess.

What was that? Skia hisses as we make a sharp right and come to a quieter, but still touristy block.

I roll to a stop, hop off the bike, and walk it to a set of black ivory twisted doors. An old wooden sign hangs from iron hooks on the brick wall; it reads *Agatha's Emporium* in fancy script.

"Don't worry about it," I grumble, trying to put the moment from my mind and focus on the entirely more important situation at hand.

Those humans made you angry?

"Yeah," I utter through gritted teeth, chaining my bike up to the convenient post a couple yards from the entrance.

I don't understand.

"I'm not a..." I heave a sigh. At no point in my coming-out stage did I think I'd have this conversation with my cat. Or a demon. "You get what binary is?"

As a concept?

"Sure. As a concept. Black and white, right and wrong, one and zero."

Heaven and hell, got it.

"Cool, I'm not binary. I'm not one or the other of the two options most of humanity uses to categorize themselves."

Ahh, yes. I see.

I squint at Skia, standing in the basket, surveying me with an unsettlingly intelligent gaze. "Do you actually?"

No, but I don't think it matters.

I shrug. "Good enough. Let's go."

Skia jumps from the basket and nearly trips me in a very cat-like move of twining around my ankles.

"Stay close to me in here. And don't knock anything over."

The demon hisses. I chuckle. The bell above the door tinkles as we step inside.

I AM A DEMON

Five

Agatha's Emporium is a dark space. Velvet and lace curtained windows, rows and rows of black bookshelves, dangling chandeliers with hints of light, and dark ivy crawling across every open surface. The plants survive on the limited light streaming through the glass door, shadows from the twisted iron designs marring the floor.

The place smells amazing. Always something new but familiar like the changing of the seasons. Pumpkins, cinnamon, nutmeg... I inhale deep, the scents warming my chest. A happy change from the stink of the city and my musty apartment.

Skia sneezes.

I glance down, raise an eyebrow, and open my mouth.

Don't.

I snort just as Agatha steps out from behind the bar-height checkout counter to the left of the entrance.

"Demi!" She grins and opens her arms. "Hug?"

"Absolutely," I return with a warm smile. It's been a while.

She pulls me in, my arms wrapping around her wide torso, thick curves on curves as she squishes me in a comforting embrace. Her curly purple and black hair cascades nearly to her waist. Fishnet covers almost every inch of skin, long sleeves hooked around her middle finger, a black skirt flaring out around her ample thighs. A dark purple vest buttons just under her breasts, leaving plenty of bosom on display.

"How are you doing?" she asks as she pulls away and bends down to pet who she thinks is Missy. "I haven't seen you in a while. Everything okay?"

"Yeah." I shrug and fiddle with the leathers on my wrist. "Don't worry about me, Ags. I've got my cat."

She rolls her eyes. "And Missy is great."

Skia jerks away from her hands, scrambling around my legs to sit behind me.

Ags raises an immaculately shaped eyebrow. "But you need human interaction, too. Beyond the grocery store."

"I've been getting groceries delivered."

Ags gives me a deadpan stare and straightens. "What's up with Missy? She feeling okay?"

I glance at the demon, currently standing on their back legs as they inspect a ceramic skull on the third shelf of a nearby display. "Yeah, she's a bit off today. Listen, I need to get a few things." I pull the list from my back pocket.

"Didn't come to hang out?" Ags sounds genuinely disappointed, and I offer a sheepish smile.

"Sorry, but I'll come by later in the week to spend some time."

"Lunch?"

I unfold the paper and pass it into her hands. “Sure, that sounds great.”

Ags sighs. “I can live with that. You buy—” She falters as her hazel eyes scan the list. “Demi... what is this all for?”

I'm about to attempt an answer when I hear Skia let out a pained hiss. I rush around a bookshelf covered in trinkets and spot them staring at an ornate cross hung above a silver inlaid mirror. I freeze as Ags’ footsteps sound behind me.

The thing in the mirror is absolutely not my cat—in a more obvious way than glowing red eyes.

Horns, black and shadowed, rise just in front of dark, elongated ears. Missy’s reflection isn’t fluffy. Instead, her fur appears short and velvety, a peach fuzz covering pale gray skin. The limbs are long, awkward, and disjoined.

I hurriedly step in front of the mirror, nudging Skia aside with my foot as I mutter, “Be more of a cliché, why don’t you,” and take the cross from the wall. I set it on a shelf as Ags steps around the corner.

“Everything okay?”

“Like I said, she’s not feeling herself today.” I turn to my friend and throw on a nonchalant smile. “So, that list?”

The crease in Ags forehead suggests completing my mission might not go well, but she just gives me a squinty, suspicious look and heads deeper into the shop.

“Nightshade and candles I can do. I’ll have to double check the back for black chalk.”

Hmph, Skia grumbles in my head. *What kind of magic shop doesn’t have black chalk*?

I wait until Ags pushes through a long black curtain to the small storage space in the back of the store before I round on Skia.

"Knock off the attitude. You should be glad she's helping. And," I shoot an incredulous glare their way, "stay away from mirrors."

Agatha pops her head out from behind the curtain, an eyebrow raised. "Who are you talking to?"

My eyes widen, and I swallow a lump in my throat. "Missy."

Ags sighs. "Human contact, Demi. Seriously."

I flash a tight, toothy grin.

She rolls her eyes and returns to her search.

Why does she speak so much of human contact? Are you not contacting enough of your species?

I glance at the black curtain before moving toward the front of the store with a gesture for Skia to follow me. I settle onto a plump emerald green armchair studded with gold.

Skia arcs in a nimble leap and perches on a small coffee table to my right. Their tail flicks along the spine of a book sitting on the glass inlaid surface. They tilt their head at me expectantly.

"Humans need..." I grit my teeth. "Humans need to be around other humans. Sometimes. For... comfort and," I blow out a sigh and wriggle in the comfortable chair, "caring. Physical contact is important. Um... conversation. We go a bit crazy if we're alone too long. There's a bunch of studies on solitary confinement that talk about how bad it is for your brain."

This seems to be an unfavorable weakness.

I blink and gaze at the demon. "Finally something we agree on."

Demons don't need company. I wandered hell alone for nearly five decades before I managed to... Skia darts a look at me as they hesitate. *Before I came through the gate.*

"Damn. That's a long time. You don't get lonely?"

Lonely?

"Yeah. I like being alone, but my life definitely got better when Missy moved in. A warm body around makes the apartment feel less empty."

Hmm. Hell is warm enough without extra bodies.

I snort, just as Agatha prances out of the back room.

"Found it!" she sings as she strides forward with a double-bagged paper sack. "This is everything on your list. Plus some sticks of cinnamon and pine I just finished drying out. Hang them on a hook and they'll make your whole place smell amazing."

I stand, shaking my head with a smile that creases my eyes. "You're too good to me, Ags." I cross to the check-out counter, pay her, and scoop up the bag. "Wednesday?"

"Don't forget this time. Keep your phone on. I'll call to remind you in the morning."

I offer up a one-armed hug, and she takes it. "I won't. I've missed you."

"You know I don't want to run out your battery, but I do worry about you all alone so often."

I shrug. Skia beats me to the door and paws at the glass for a moment before turning to glower at me.

"I've got Missy."

Agatha shakes her head. "See you Wednesday."

Six

Skia darts out the door as I push it open with one hand, the other clutching my bag of witchy stuff that's supposed to help me exorcize my cat.

"You'll have to ride on my shoulder," I say as I gently nestle the bag into the basket at the front of my bike.

No more an insult to my pride than riding in that monstrosity, Skia grumbles.

I cackle as I bend to undo the lock and chain.

"Hey!"

My breath hitches. Like a bucket of ice water was upended onto my shoulders, a slam of cold runs down my spine. I swallow, set my jaw, and turn.

The misgendering jerks from before stalk forward from the end of the alley. Just my luck they happen to be passing by right when I leave Agatha's.

My hand tightens around the chain I'm holding. The bike is propped in the metal bike post. I walk around it, listening to the nagging voice in my head telling me not to turn my back on these guys.

With quick fingers, I loop the chain around the seat and pull the bike clear of the pole. The men are closer.

My heartbeat pisses me off. It should be calm. Steady. They're only men.

I glance at Skia. "Hop up. Let's get outta here."

Skia bounds onto the seat and then my shoulder. *Is everything all right?*

"Where are you going, sweetie?"

I grimace and say nothing, to Skia or the men now only a few yards away.

I make to swing a leg over the bike. One of the men darts forward and grabs the handlebars, yanking just enough that I stumble and don't manage to get on. Skia slips from my shoulder with a soft yowl. They land on their feet and circle my ankles again.

"Let go of my bike," I growl.

"Aww, come on, honey. You don't need to be like that. I just wanna talk."

My flesh crawls. The scowl on my lips grows, the furrow in my brow expressing my fury and discomfort. Not that they care.

"Ha." Another of them laughs. "Since when do you go for guys?"

"What?" Confusion flashes across the face of the one holding my bike. He looks at his friend, then back at me with a curled lip. "Aren't you a girl?"

"I'm neither, asshole. Let go of my bike."

The air shifts. A weight comes down as their faces change, warp as confusion and malice replace the fun time they thought they were having before.

The one holding my handlebars yanks again, and my grip on the seat slips. He shoves the bike over. It clangs to the ground. A bundle of green falls from the top of the paper bag, a few pieces of orange and black striped tissue paper are picked up by the breeze.

He steps forward, and I square my shoulders, raising my jaw.

His hand slams into my sternum. I hit the wall behind me with an oomph and a grunt.

"Back off," I manage through gritted teeth.

My ears ring. Whatever they're saying—they're all talking now, words pouring out and trying to weigh me down like wet cement—I can't hear them. All I hear is the pounding of my blood and my breath.

The man's mouth moves, utters something inconsequential as he pulls back a fist, and I brace for the swing.

He freezes.

I blink and step to the side. He doesn't move. I step again, my gaze sliding from his immobile form to the men behind him.

They aren't moving either. Their mouths are open, curses and insults hanging on their breath.

Then I notice their eyes.

Their eyes *are* moving. Wide and terrified and...

I take a step forward, squinting for a second before I stumble back in horror.

Black oozes from their eyes. Tears of darkness, stinking of sulfur, drip down their faces and fall to the ground. The asphalt sizzles.

"What..." I breathe.

That was a mistake.

I know Skia's voice isn't only echoing in my head, because the eyes of the men around me widen even further. I glance at the demon cat. They've changed, morphed Missy's body to look more like the creature I saw in the mirror. Not quite that level of terrifying, but definitely not a cat anymore.

The ground shakes. I take a few steps back, putting the wall at my back as Skia deliberately circles the men.

One you will pay for... with your lives.

The guttural hiss with which Skia speaks sends fresh chills down my spine. One of the men breaks from his paralysis and falls to his knees with a whimper. He wipes at his eyes and lets out a sob as his fingers come away coated in black ooze.

"Skia," I murmur, sure they can hear me even as the wind picks up around us, the ground groaning and shifting. "They don't need... I think this is enough for them to learn their lesson. You don't need to kill them."

Need? Skia looks back at me, that angular body disjointed and sharp. The contacts fell out with the transformation, and their red eyes glint with unnatural light. ***Who said anything about need? These men ought to die simply because I wish it.***

The one on the ground screams and scurries to his feet. Panting and sobbing, he races to the end of the alley, stumbling on the cracked, uneven asphalt.

"Skia," I say again, my voice soft against the roaring earth and air. "Let them go. This isn't right."

Let them... Skia falters. Their form shrinks as they look to me. ***They hurt you. They wanted to hurt you more.***

"But they didn't. You stopped them."

The form shrinks more, becoming the tiny black cat I recognize. *I did.*

"Thank you."

Skia give a slow blink, the red of their eyes disappearing for a long second. When their eyes open again, whatever holds the men in place breaks. They scatter, leaving behind a scent of fear and piss.

You're... Skia swallows and gives a swish of their tail. *You're welcome.*

"What the hell was that?"

I wheel around. Agatha is standing at her shop, the door propped open, a phone in her hand. Her eyes are round, fear on her face.

"Uh..." I glance at Skia and bend to pick up the things that fell from my bike basket. I tuck them into the paper and lift my bike off the ground.

"I called the cops, Demi. Those guys..."

Her gaze darts to Skia, then back at me.

The fear on her face has shifted to something different. Excitement. Curiosity.

My mouth twitches up into a smile. "Like I said, you don't need to worry about me. I've got my cat." I jerk my head at Skia. They take three looping steps, jump onto the bike-seat, and then to my shoulder.

I swing my leg over the bike, wave to Ags, and begin to pedal us home.

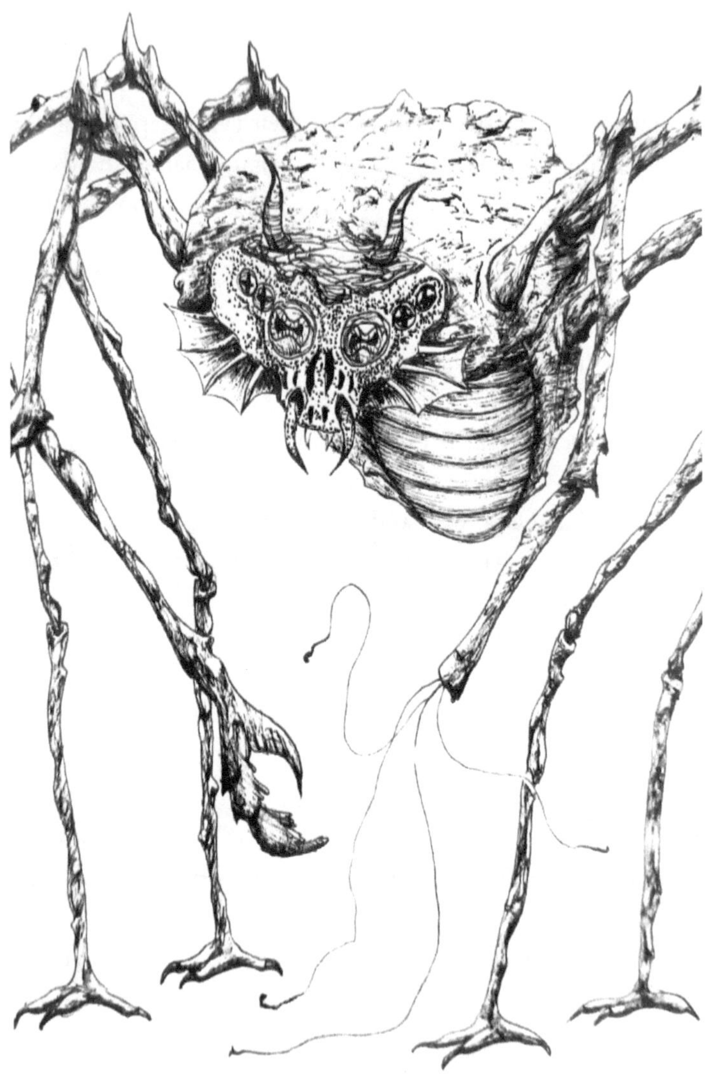

Seven

I take the long way back: narrow alleys, no tourists, limited people. We pass a few unhoused persons, a cop, and a lot of trash. I make a sharp turn only a few blocks from my building and zip down a dark street. Light shines on a two-lane thoroughfare at the end, but the buildings on either side of us are too high for any sunlight beyond an hour in the middle of the day.

We're maybe twenty yards from the T intersection at the end of the alley when the air shudders. Warps. I slow to a stop, heartbeat racing.

"Was that you?"

Skai swallows, the sound audible as their throat is right next to my ear. *No.*

I wait, jaw tight and back tense. There. Where sunlight meets the shadows, the ground begins to sink.

A pit of molten rock stretches out, maybe five feet in diameter. Hooked sludge-green claws grasp the edges.

The heavy weight of fear drags at my stomach, pulling me down, rooting me to the spot.

No, no, no, Skia mutters, trembling on my shoulder.

"Skia, what's..."

Words leave me. Thought leaves me as the creature before us pulls itself from the ground. The long, narrow claws connect to insect-like arms, bent in three places like a spider with an extra joint. Almost as many of them, too. It plants five claws onto the asphalt and lifts its body.

Bile builds in my throat.

As dry and skeletal as the arms are, its lumpy body drips with sludge—a familiar black ooze that sizzles where it falls on the street. The head is mangled. Six eyes—that I can see—two at the front, two on each side. Not human, not by a long shot, but not insect either. Maybe similar to a rat, with the elongated nose and pointed teeth, but the ears are twisted up like a candy-cane. Like something gripped the ends with pliers and spun them in circles.

It looks beyond painful.

Then again, maybe those aren't the ears. As fear curdles in my belly, sending shudders down my spine, I note black slits between the sets of eyes. Maybe the things on its head are horns.

Foolish thing.

I exhale a breath of terror. This thing doesn't speak like Skia, a soft murmuring hiss in my head. This thing's words echo, reverberating through my skull and sticking to the walls of my brain with painful burs.

Do not speak, Skia's voice follows, so quiet compared to the thing before us.

Thinking you could escape? Leave your place?

The being approaches, leaving the sunlight and stepping onto the sidewalk. Its claws click against the cement. The pit behind it shrinks and disappears.

I did not escape, Nexus, Skia says.

I don't know if I'm supposed to hear this, too. A car drives by. A woman walks past on the far side of the street. Confusion ripples through me. Why do they not stop? Stare? Scream?

I'd scream. If I could make my throat work again.

I slipped out while you were busy. Didn't want to bother you.

The response is one of spitting fury. White glints in the thing's—Nexus's—eyes. Pinpricks of light in the bulbous shining black spheres on its head.

How dare you? I have been the gatekeeper for a thousand-thousand years. You were ***forbidden****, little shadow.*

I wince as the words slam into me. *Little shadow*, said with such derision, such scorn that my throat starts working again only to utter a furious growl.

Skia's tail strokes down my back, shooing some of the fear from my spine.

I'm not going back, Nexus.

You'll go back, shadow. You're not meant for freedom. You're meant for the pits of hell, just like the rest of us. I will pry you from that horrid form as slowly as the Drakons skin a sinner. And when we get back home, you will learn pain well enough to stop you from making such a mistake again.

It steps forward, each of the five claws scratching the ground. My mind clicks now, forming thoughts beyond the situation at hand. Ahead of it. Trying to figure out if I'll be able to swing the bike around and gather speed before Nexus is on us. Passing it is out of the question. Those legs... I don't want to know how long they reach when fully extended.

You can't escape me. Not on those weak, bipedal legs.

I barely have time to blink in confusion before Skia hisses on my shoulder. An audible, out-loud hiss as their claws contract, the pressure comforting against the fabric of my sweater.

You will not touch the human, Skia snaps.

There is a pause. A hesitation as the dots of white in Nexus's eyes flick from me to Skia and back to me again. I shudder.

Oh. A chuckle, sharp and chilling as wind ripping across an icy surface. *Ah, I see. Oh, shadow. What a failure you are. Though perhaps that beasty is fitting for you. A small thing. Worthless.*

Fury slams into me. Hot and fierce, a flame against the frozen fear I've felt since Nexus emerged from the pit. Skia coils against my neck.

My lip curls in a snarl. "Shut up."

It speaks? Brave... The rat-like head tilts, a glob of ooze falling to the ground and leaving a rutted dent in the sidewalk. *Do you know what we do to the 'brave' in hell, human? We scrub the rough edges with sandpaper until all the brave is scraped away, and the only thing left is smooth fear.* Its nose lifts into the air and sniffs. *Delicious, tender fear.*

I put a foot on the pedal, readying myself to swing around.

Something slams into Nexus. There's a flash of green, white, and flailing legs as the insect-like demon flips in the air and lands on its back.

"Damnit, Trent!"

My jaw drops, and my eye twitches as another rent-a-scooter rolls over one of Nexus's outstretched legs, loses balance, and falls to the side.

A build-up of scooters, demon body-parts, and young men in kaki pants and polos, clumps on the sidewalk where the alley meets the road.

"It wasn't me, Cody." The guy on the first scooter scrambles to his feet, sandals flapping against his heels. "The scooter got tripped up on something."

"There's nothing for it to trip up on but your yeti feet," another snaps.

Their conversation fades to the back of my attention as Nexus utters a sigh in my head, twitches, and fades into smoke.

We have to go. Now.

I nod, flip the bike, and pedal us toward my apartment. "What was that, Skia?"

Nexus. Keeper of the sneeze gate.

"Sneeze gate?" I repeat with less amusement and more incredulity.

There are many ways to enter your world, Demi. The sneeze gate is one. The most active one at times.

"Why, exactly," I huff, pumping my legs until they burn and taking turns far faster than I normally would, "is the sneeze gate keeper after you?"

It is possible that I did not get the authority of my superiors before... uh... slipping through the gate.

"You—" huff— "snuck—" huff— "out of hell?"

When you put it like that... yes.

Eight

"What just happened?" I ask after I've slowed down a little, giving myself the ability to breathe again. "Did those guys destroy that thing?"

Not in the slightest. Nexus was momentarily tangled, and likely thought shadowing out was the fastest way to get himself undone.

"Why did..." I gulp, glancing behind us for the twentieth time as I turn onto our street. "Why could I see it—him, and no one else could?"

Because he thought I was in you. Had he known my form from the start, it's unlikely he'd have let you. Demons do not like being seen by mortals. It puts them on their guard.

"You can say that again." I slow to a stop at the door of the apartment building. "Do you..." Skia jumps from my shoulder. I use my keycode on the door, push it open, and follow the demon inside. "Do you look like that?"

Nothing so fierce. Skia glances back with a somewhat sheepish expression on Missy's face. *Shadow demons are the smallest of our kind. My true form is... petite.*

If I wasn't still scared out of my mind, I'd laugh. As it is, a smile crosses my face. I heft the paper bag and make for the stairs, Skia on my heels.

My phone rings halfway up. It's Ags. I send it to voicemail and put the ringer on silent. I will call her. After I get Skia out of my cat.

I fumble with the lock, fingers still trembling from our encounter.

"Okay." I set the bag on the shoved-aside coffee table. "What now?"

Start by drawing the shapes I gave you with black chalk across the floorboards.

"How long..." I get my notebook and the sticky notes and quickly draw the complicated lines Skia explained before we left. "How did he find you?"

I was foolish.

"That doesn't answer my question."

Skia hisses, smudges a section of chalk with his padded paws, and directs me to redo it at a slightly different angle. *I used my demonic powers. They can be traced.*

"Will he be able to tell when you go into someone new?"

I... I'm not sure. Nexus did not come here. He did not know I was in this form. I believe I have to use a deeper power for him to track me.

I finish off the chalk circle with a flourish. "No pentagrams?"

Skia rolls their eyes. *Not everything hellish needs a pentagram, Demi.*

I shrug. "So we get you out of Missy, you enter a different body, and... what? Nexus just leaves?"

Once you are no longer harboring me, Nexus will be unable to harm you without facing severe punishment in hell. I believe when he has lost the trail, he will return to his post.

I pause in the middle of placing nightshade in little clusters around the drawing. "You believe? What if he doesn't leave?"

He will leave.

"How do you know?"

Because when you send me back to hell, he will follow.

I freeze. Heat goes through my chest. "What do you mean, back to hell?"

He's found me. When I'm in a larger, more capable form, it will be harder to hide my demonic powers.

"Your powers are limited by the cat body?" I set the candles out.

Infuriating, isn't it?

"But you don't have to go back, do you? I thought we were just doing the first half of this. You'll find a different body."

At my most powerful, I might be able to fight Nexus and survive. But beating him? Out of the question. Besides...

Skia's tail swishes. They nudge a candle half an inch to the left.

"Besides what?"

If I stay in this realm, it is possible Nexus could make a claim that you are still... caring for me. You have to send me back.

I open my mouth to argue, but a strange scent hits my nostrils. The stench of rotting meat, blown through the open window.

I rise and walk to the sill, leaning out just enough to see the sidewalk on the busy street below.

A shudder races down my spine. I jerk back and slam the window closed, fiddling with the little lock a moment too long before it finally slides into place.

Demi?

"He's here." My mouth is dry. My fingers shake. I run across the small apartment to the door and slide the chain across.

That's not going to stop a gatekeeper from hell, Demi.

"Better than nothing," I snap.

Start the ritual. I will do what I can.

Nine

I frown at the cat-demon and return to kneel at the edge of the sigil. Fresh blood is the last thing, beyond the words I have to sound out.

I gulp. I don't like pain. Never have, never will. No masochists over here.

I pick up the cheese knife I cleaned before we left for Agatha's. My hand quivers over my arm.

Something slams into my door.

I nearly fall over. Eyes wide, my gaze darts to Skia—standing a few feet from the door and staring at it with furious intensity—before I pierce my skin. Blood drips, too slowly. With a wince and a moan, I widen the gash a few inches from my wrist on the top part of my arm.

I toss away the blade. Blood dribbles now. Enough that I can dip two fingers into the red sludge and trace the symbols that require it.

Another slam against the door.

I jerk back from the sigil, grasp for a strip of gauze I laid out earlier, and wrap it around my arm.

Then I lift my notebook off the floor and begin to read.

The words come slow, halting, and thick on my tongue. I don't speak this language. The words are written so I can read it aloud.

I have no idea what I'm saying.

I can't hold him much longer, Skia hisses. They step back. Once, twice, a third time until their back legs are at the edge of the chalk outline. *Once the first part of the incantation is done, Missy will be free from me. Keep her out of the circle. If she steps in during the second half, she might be sent with me.*

An ache creeps through my chest as I nod, hesitating. I've reached the last few lines of the first section. Skia backs a little further.

The door cracks. A jagged hunk of wood chips off the center. Nexus's long, sharp teeth glint through the opening.

Finish it, Skia says.

I do.

The air picks up. Wind swirling through the apartment, though none of the windows are open. The candles flicker but don't go out. The flames grow, rising two, three inches from the wicks as rumbling fills the space.

Skia—Missy—yowls in the center of the sigil.

I scramble back, the notebook clenched in my fingers as I press against the wall bisecting my apartment. Nexus continues to pound on the door, but my gaze is stuck on my friends.

Harsh sounds fill the air: ripping, tearing, scratching. Softer ones as well; a whimper, a cry.

Missy darts from the sigil, brushes by my ankle, and disappears under the pushed-aside loveseat.

There, left in the center of the chalk and blood and candles... a tiny black shadow.

Skia's form *is* petite. About Missy's size, even a little smaller. Darker than night, but warm. Like the coals left over after a fire burns out.

They open their eyes. The same glowing red that stared at me through Missy stares at me now.

"Are you..." I don't know what to ask. Are you okay? Are you sure about going back to hell?

Finish it, Skia snaps.

The same voice, still whispering in my head.

Missy yowls from under the couch.

The door splinters open. Wood slams against the wall, one of the hinges cracks, and the door hangs off its side.

Nexus stalks into the room; his nails click against the hardwood floor.

A shudder runs down my spine. I lift the notebook and continue the ritual. Only three lines left.

Missy yowls again and crawls out from under the couch.

Two lines. My throat is dry.

Say the name. That's the important part. Make sure you say the name...

One line left.

Missy's familiar yellow eyes meet mine.

Nexus approaches. Looms over Skia.

They shrink inward. Wince away from the claws reaching out to drag them back to hell.

Nexus spares a glance at me. A pitiless, bottomless black gaze that drills me to the spot.

Missy yowls one more time—launches off her hindlegs; I say the last word, and everything goes dark.

Ten

Swirling black smoke consumes my apartment. Shrieking, endless voices screaming, flames and ash lick up from the sides of a pit in my living room, growing to the size of the sigil.

Nexus stands over the pit. Confusion fogs his eyes. The ground before him trembles as it sinks inward. There's a split second of time as he looks around for his prey.

His claw, about to sink into the shadowy form of Skia, now hangs over empty air. Across from me, pressed against the wall, is my little cat.

Missy, having leapt from her place by the couch as I uttered that final word... her body covering the demon.

Nexus screams. Shrill and violent and terrible as he falls, grasping at the sides of the floor for traction. But none is found.

I said his name. I did the ritual correctly. Even if there were chains binding him to the room, he'd still be sinking into hell.

A moment passes and the screaming fades. The floor closes up. There's a mess of chalk, blood, and candle wax, but no pit to the abyss, so I'm gonna call it a win.

What... Skia slides out from under Missy. Their movement is fluid, gliding across the floor. *What did you do?*

I brush back the sweaty hair clinging to my forehead and take a deep breath. "Well, you said the name is the important part. He only found you cuz you used your powers. It's not like he knows the mortal plane very well..." My eyes go wide with a moment of panic. "Right? He said it had been thousands of years. He doesn't like... know what street we're on, does he?"

No... Skia stares, from me to Missy and back again.

Missy pads up to them and rubs her back against their shadowy form the same way she does to my ankles.

Why did you do that?

I swallow, finally pushing up from the floor as I stride across to the mangled front door. I glance back at them. "Why did you stop those guys from hurting me?"

I...

The shadow seems lost for words. Their red eyes narrow, no eyebrows to furrow or expression to read, but they stutter for a moment before falling silent.

"Listen," I say, pitifully scraping the door closed. A new one won't be cheap, but if I can get Ags to help, I might be able to install it before the landlord finds out. "I get that you wanted to find a new body to possess, but you also said that's a good way for Nexus to find you."

Missy approaches as I turn to face the room. I bend and scoop, cradling her in my arms. She puts a paw on my shoulder and rubs her head against my chest.

"I was thinking..." I swallow, scratching behind her ears. "If you want to, that is... but you might stay with us for a while." I gesture at the wreck of an apartment before Missy puts her paw on my hand and drags me back to giving her scratchies. "There's plenty of room. I can get some blackout curtains for the windows if you need dark places to be during the day or something."

You'd... continue to harbor me?

"Sure. You're not the worst company. And Missy clearly likes you."

Missy purrs in my arms, wiggles, and launches off of me, landing lightly on the ground. She flicks Skia with her tail as she makes her way to the windowsill. A moment later, she's back in her usual perch, curled up and enjoying the sun.

I chuckle. "We are gonna have to tell Ags about you. I hope that's okay. She's been calling me nonstop since we left the shop." I pull my phone out. It hasn't stopped vibrating since I turned the sound off. "You okay if I tell her to come over?"

I suppose... I suppose that would be fine, as long as she promises to leave her crosses at the store.

"I don't think that'll be a problem. In fact, I bet once she meets you, she'll take them down permanently."

Why?

"Because she's gonna like you as much as I do."

A week later finds the four of us at my apartment. Chinese food containers litter the kitchen counter, the smell of egg foo young being aired out via the open window.

Missy sits in her basket, content and seemingly unfazed by her short stint as a demon's body.

Ags and I laugh at the table, cracking open the dozen fortune cookies we got from the restaurant. The front door is fixed. A new hunk of wood in place, complete with a few sigils burned into the bottom.

Skia sits on their own perch at the top of the wall covered in plants, munching on an egg roll. The greenery offers enough shade that they don't get uncomfortable from all the light. They are a shadow after all, and shadows don't last long in the sun.

The apartment seems bigger these days. Pockets of darkness hide my new friend during the day, and at night they can't seem to leave the window. Just the sliver of sky visible from our spot on the fourth floor is enough. They stare at the stars until the sun comes up.

Ags and I are planning a trip out of the city in a little while. We could use a break from the traffic, the noise. Let Missy run through some tall grass. Let Skia see the sky without all the light pollution.

I meet Skia's red eyes with a wide grin and toss up another spring roll. A tendril of black shadow grasps it out of the air.

I lean back in my chair, my gaze falling briefly on the scab across my arm. A small price to pay. One I'd pay again.

After all, that's what you do for a friend.

Book Two
One Hell of a Road Trip

One

Preparing for a road trip is a tricky procedure. Having to bear in mind that a demon who guards a gate of hell is constantly on the hunt for one of your best friends while preparing for a road trip, is harder.

Add on the fact that we're bringing my tiny black cat and that we're on a time crunch, and the "relaxing time away from the city" that Agatha promised is looking more and more like a stressful next week and a half.

"I'm just saying," I utter through gritted teeth. "If I can't get these window shades to stick, it might make sense for you to stay home."

Skia, a shadowy demon who spent the last five-hundred years in hell, somehow narrows their red eyes. How, you ask? No clue. My friend is the incarnation of demonic energy with no capsule. They often remind me of thick black smoke—if smoke was sentient.

The little black form bounces. *I'll not stay behind, Demi. This city is large, but I crave more. I dream of conquering the rest of this land.*

I snort. At the trunk of the car, Ags does the same. She pops her head up from where she's been Tetris-ing our luggage. Vibrant purple streaks in her hair shine in the faint beam of streetlight coming down a block away. It's hard to pack at night, but too much light hurts Skia.

Hence the window shades.

"Skia," Ags says, humor in her tone, "is 'conquering' the right word? Or do you mean seeing? Seeing the rest of this land is very different than conquering it."

Skia shifts, their shadowy body wrapped around the headrest, to turn those beady eyes on Ags. *I said what I meant.*

"And when exactly did you conquer Denver?" I ask with a smirk on my lips. "I don't keep up on the news much; I must have missed it."

Ags lets out a barking laugh and shoves one last box into the trunk.

We wouldn't have as much crap in this little rental car, but we aren't just attending this wedding; Agatha is officiating it.

For traditional folks, that would mean bringing some religious text and maybe a laptop. For Ags' cousin and her groom-to-be, it means Ags is lugging half of her witchy/wiccan gear to the east coast.

We also have to get there a day early to help set up.

None of which I mind. My issue stems from trying to stop Skia burning up in daylight while we are driving. And trying to stop Missy from flipping out and shredding her car carrier.

Problems for the morning, Demi. Skia murmurs, their voice in my mind only.

I sigh. With a grunt, I'm able to get the shade fixed into place, and I turn to my demonic friend. "How do you do that?"

The shadow bounces on the seat, a gesture I've taken to be a shrug. *You aren't as hard to read as you think, my friend.*

"Or you're in my head."

Skia scoffs. *I'd never betray your trust in such a way.*

I raise my eyebrows, crossing my arms with incredulity.

Well, and I can't use my power or the demons from hell will find me. Talking to you privately takes some of my own effort, but reading your mind is beyond my personal capacity.

This response is more believable. I know it to be true, and I'm glad Skia has been so careful. The thought of coming face to face with Nexus, a gatekeeper of hell bent on dragging my friend back to the underworld, stirs snakes of anxiety in my gut. We went head-to-head once before. That was almost six months ago, when Skia first arrived on this plane.

Missy and I sent Nexus back to hell empty-handed—proving how smart cats are and guaranteeing that I have extra-dimensional enemies I never could have imagined before a demon possessed my cat.

Part of the ritual to banish Nexus also released Skia from the confines of Missy's body. Now I have two balls of black living in my studio apartment with me.

At least only one of them needs to use the litter box.

"Double latte, americano, and two puppy cups."

The barista hands over our drinks. I thank her and am about to roll up the window when she asks, "I see one kitty, but where is the other one?"

A low hissing chuckle sounds from the floor of the back seat.

"The other one is shy," I reply with a smile.

In the passenger seat, comfortably tucked into a Buffy the Vampire Slayer blanket, Ags chuckles. I pass her the drinks, give the barista a nod, and pull away from the drive-thru.

We're on our way. Four days, over a dozen states, and several downloaded audiobooks and podcasts ready to go. I pull up the first campaign of NADDPOD (Not Another D&D Podcast) since Ags has yet to listen to it.

Skia moves under my seat, the edge of their shadow popping up between my legs, and I hand them a cup of whipped cream. *Turn it up,* they hiss. *This is my favorite part.*

Missy yowls in agreement—or anger—until Ags tucks the second cup into her crate.

Two

My favorite part of the drive is early morning. I've got my coffee, low music, and there is minimal traffic. After a few hours, Ags takes over the driving, and I focus on getting some homework done.

Was it Skia showing up that made me want to enroll in some online classes and start working towards my degree in World Religions? Maybe. Maybe it was explaining the whole situation to Ags, which led to her hanging around my apartment more. Which made my desire to have as little as possible to do with the outside world lessen—slightly.

Turns out human contact *is* important. I'm sure I'd be fine with just Skia and Missy, but as we blow past a billboard advertising Easter family dinners at some chain restaurant, I can't help the swell of gratitude I feel for Ags.

"Hey," I mutter. "Thanks for bringing us to this."

Agatha raises an immaculately penciled in eyebrow. When she had time to do them, I have no clue. We spent last night in a motel, and I'm pretty sure she was asleep until the very last moment possible this morning.

"Of course." She grins and glances into the backseat. Skia is beside Missy's crate, their shadowy form settled onto the cushions with an odd stretch of neck rising up so they can look out the shade-covered window. "Can't let Skia live without seeing more of the world, Demi."

Ags' gaze catches on me as she turns back to the road. I'm sure she's thinking the same thing about me. In the few years we've known each other, she's never seen me leave the city.

I lean up against the door, enjoying the comfortability of this little rental. The view is stunning. Nonstop rolling hills, still green from the precipitation from winter. Flowers grow among the tall grass, dotting the landscape with color.

I used to live in a place like this.

I like the city.

Skia's favorite part of the drive is nighttime. I get behind the wheel again, and they sit on my lap, staring out the windshield with all the attention a new world deserves.

Why so many lights? they ask as we pull off the interstate and head toward our Airbnb.

I chuckle. "East coast. Big cities mean big lights."

And this... east coast... has many large metropolitan areas?

"Yeah. But there are plenty of places with more nature. We can find some hiking or something tomorrow."

I pull into the driveway of a petite house with a cute wrap-around porch and twinkling lights. Skia moves up onto my shoulder, away from the light coming in through my window.

There have always been trees, Demi. I have less interest in nature and more in the marvels of humankind.

"That's... that's a really nice way to put it. We'll try to find some marvels for you."

Ags grins over at me. "That shouldn't be too hard, Skia. I have a few places in mind for us to visit tomorrow."

I raise an eyebrow as we step out of the car. "What places?"

She runs a hand through her dark hair with a chuckle. "Witchy places."

With no further explanation, and therefore leaving me completely bewildered, she grabs her overnight bag and heads to the door to type in the code and let us all in.

I get Missy's crate from the back. She's done well so far, but she definitely prefers the solitude of her cushy box to the open air of the car. Skia slips into the big hood of my sweatshirt, hanging down at the base of my neck. They flick my hair around and are soon entirely shrouded in darkness.

"Comfy back there?" I ask.

Indeed.

"What are you going to do when I cut my hair?" I laugh, carrying us all into the cozy house. Skia weighs almost nothing, except when they're wet. Oddly enough the shadow that makes up their form is really absorbent.

The low hiss of Skia's chuckle echoes in my mind as we go in, locate a take-out menu for a nearby pizza place, and order dinner.

"So," I mumble through a mouthful of pepperoni. "What witchy spot are we going to tomorrow? I thought we were in a bit of a hurry?"

Ags leans across the round dining table in the middle of the kitchen and grabs a slice of garlic bread. "We're a few hours from Salem."

I scrunch my nose, feeding a bit of pepperoni to Missy as she curls around my ankles. "Isn't that a *bad* place to be a witch?"

Ags rolls her eyes. "At one time, yes. Now, it's a tourist attraction. I think it'd be a fun spot. Plus, we might find something cute for my cousin. I'm not sold on the wine glasses I picked out."

Surely not, Skia says, a slice of pizza disappearing into their shadowy form. *It only took you two weeks to decide on that particular set.*

"And that was after you went with glasses instead of candlesticks," I add.

Ags gives us both a squinty glare. "Shaddup."

The three of us share a round of chuckles, and Missy yowls for more scraps.

"Salem it is," I say with a grin at my friends. "But if anyone lights any matches, we're outta there."

Three

Salem Massachusetts is an annoyingly beautiful town. For a place where so much awful stuff happened, it's startlingly quaint.

Missy surprises me by staying on Ags' shoulder. She really adds to my friend's already highly witchy aesthetic. Flowing black skirts with violet and green embroidery, an "everyday" corset—as she calls it—thick eyeliner and mascara, and blood red lipstick already make her look like she walked out of a sequel to Practical Magic. Missy brings an element of mystery, and a touch of cuteness, to the whole ensemble.

Skia and I are a different story. I'm in my usual jeans and a comfy oversized hoodie. Skia stirs fitfully in the big pocket. Bits of their form ooze out the sides, making it look like my hands are smoking. They shift around.

Turn a bit, Demi. I want to see that.

I roll my eyes with a grin and move sideways so Skia can get a glimpse of the multi-passenger bike thing touristy places like this have.

They ride as one, Skia says.

A few steps ahead of me, Ags pauses to see what Skia is talking about. She cackles as the bike goes around a corner. "I've been on one of those before. Half of my cousins only pretended to pedal."

Ahh, falsifiers. They shall be rightly punished when their time on this plane ends.

I open my mouth, meet Ags' eye, and close it again. Skia has been here for a while now but still terrifies me with what they say half the time. Well, sort of terrifies. It's like watching a gruesome comedy. I often don't know if I should laugh or be utterly horrified.

"Nah." Ags spares me the task of having to respond. "They're good guys. This was back when we were teenagers. Everyone's a dumbass as a teenager."

At this I do chuckle, nodding in agreement as Skia's head briefly pops out of my pocket to look up at me.

Your species is strange.

"Buddy, you have no idea." I glance up the street, and my heart swells at the sight of a café sign a block away. "Coffee?"

Ags shakes her head, gently shifting Missy to her other shoulder. "You've gotta break this habit, Demi."

"No," I say with a grin, darting ahead of her as Skia hisses protests about being jostled. "I really don't."

The coffee is hot, the pastry is fresh, and Skia is safely tucked behind me in the corner of our booth seat. The cold of their shadow caresses my shoulder as they eye my blueberry scone.

This little shop is as cute as the rest of the town. Lights hang at even intervals, casting shadows in odd shapes. If it weren't so crowded, I'd love to watch Skia dance through them like a cat burglar going through lasers. It's a game we play at home a lot.

But there are people at almost every table and the line is out the door.

Ags settles next to me after a five-minute wait for her drink, and she looks like she stepped in something rotten on the way over.

Missy jumps from her shoulder to also beg for pieces of my scone. I should have gotten two.

"What's wrong?" I wince as I sip the scalding coffee, but the warmth is so lovely as it spreads through my chest and belly that I care less about my slightly burnt tongue.

Ags shakes her head. With an angry expression still in place, she separates one of the many chains around her neck, pulling forth a purple crystal.

"Ags?" I prompt. I'm usually the one too distracted or spaced out to answer a question.

"That barista," she snaps.

I raise an eyebrow, noting the steam coming from Ags' mug. "It took a couple minutes, but your drink is still hot. What's the issue?"

Skia cocks the portion of shadow that is their head. "*Perhaps her scone is not as delectable as ours.*"

"Ours?" I scowl. "I specifically asked if you wanted anything before I ordered. You said no."

Hmph. I ought to try Agatha's scone. To check. Missy agrees.

My scowl becomes a snort as I break off a chunk of scone and raise it to my shoulder. It disappears from my fingers. Missy is next, and I give her a sizably smaller piece to avoid tummy issues later.

I think she notices, because when she kneads my leg her claws go deeper than usual.

Ags has ignored the entire conversation. She holds the crystal—amethyst, I think—to her lips and mutters against the stone.

"Ags, what's going on?"

"That woman is messed up."

I look to the front of the shop where the barista is laughing along with a customer about something.

"What happened?"

She shakes her head, finishes whatever chanting she was doing with the crystal, and lets it fall back to her chest. "She asked if I'm a witch."

I purse my lips, then lift my mug to avoid saying the wrong thing and wait for her to continue.

"That's not the problem." Ags flails a heavily ringed hand. "But when I told her I'm Wiccan she went off on me."

I frown. "That's crazy. Why?"

"She said Wiccans aren't real casters, and we're a white-washed version of witches and that we give the whole magical community a bad name."

I sip my coffee.

For all the strange supernatural stuff I've seen since Skia possessed Missy, I have yet to witness any sort of human witchy/wiccan magic actually work.

Sure, there is manifesting what you want in life, there are candles that have scents to help someone relax, and I'm sure meditation is a beneficial part of the spell casting process. But actual magic? Like, lighting candles with a fingertip, or making things float, or any of the stuff seen in Hollywood... that's all continued to be fiction.

I don't say any of that to Ags. "That's a crazy thing to say to someone. Especially someone you don't know."

She nods, her cheeks still flushed.

"Umm, what *is* the difference between witch and wicca?" I ask tentatively.

Wiccans primarily use good magic. They work toward peace and generally avoid the darker curses and spells that would cause ruin.

Ags, who had opened her mouth to respond, stares at Skia. "That's true."

And witches have a history of aiming for power. They use whatever magic is at their disposal to get what they want, damn the consequences.

I nibble on my scone. "How do you know that?"

A feeling similar to a shrug. *I spent a lot of time on earth back in the day. I've known my share of witches. And I pay attention when Ags does her rituals.*

I flush, knowing full well that I do *not* pay attention when Ags gets her incense going around my apartment.

Ags sighs, her anger melting into a satisfied smile. "All of that is correct, Skia. So the idea that someone wants to claim being a witch, let alone scold me for being wiccan, is absolute garbage."

"Agreed." I look at the barista with new eyes, irritated at the way she's made my friend feel. "Well, now we know for the return trip."

Ags raises an eyebrow, and I grin.

"We'll find a different coffee shop when we head back home."

She shakes her head but laughs. On either side of me, tiny black creatures steal the last of my scone.

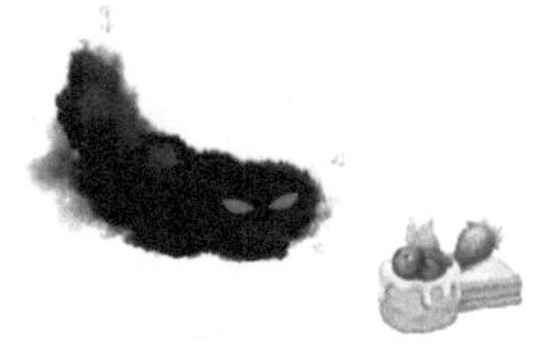

Four

We get one of those over-hyped tours after our coffee break. Ags holds a little notebook, jotting down information about her favorite spots so she can incorporate them into the map mural she wants to paint in her shop. It's going to be a large project with how many ideas she has, but I'm excited to help her get started.

I trail behind the rest of the tour group—Ags and Missy, a Dutch couple, and a handful of college students—to keep Skia out of sight. I'm a bit warm in my sweatshirt, but taking it off requires finding a dark space to keep my demon pal out of the sun while I do it. In the meantime, Skia stirs restlessly as the tour guide stops yet again to point out another building.

This one might serve our purpose. The group strides into the red and white barn and wanders for a bit. I've spent my share of time in barns, and this one is clearly for tourism. The loft is far too clean, and the equipment is ancient.

The guide goes off on a spiel about the history of the building, and I duck out of the cluster of people following her. Skia and I head behind a line of old tractors, and I take off my sweater.

Interesting.

Skia slides off my shoulder and into the scattered strands of too-clean hay.

"What?" I murmur. I bunch up the sweatshirt so they can hide in the folds when we go back into the light.

An old symbol," Skia says. "*I don't recall...*

They swirl around, sending the hay to the side as though with a breeze, and reveal a black, painted pattern on the concrete floor.

"Looks like a pentagram." I crouch for a better look. It's similar enough to the five-pointed star, but there are added details that I don't recognize. Almost hieroglyphics.

Not a pentagram. Skia's exasperation comes through the low hiss in my head. *Something else.*

"Demi?"

I wave my hand at Skia, and they hurry back to the bundle in my arms. I stand and turn as Ags comes around the tractors with a raised eyebrow.

"Everyone is moving on."

"Yep, coming. Just had to take off my sweatshirt." I gesture to the bundle of fabric and shadow in my arms and then follow Ags and the rest of the tour.

When the tour ends—and I have way too much information about burning women and the significance of mushrooms in my head—we make our way back to the little hostel we're staying in.

Ags booked us a private room with two beds. We fill up on bulky sandwiches and tea. Skia steals most of my ice cream, while Ags happily shares hers with Missy.

"Two days out," I say, stretching out on my bed and staring up at the popcorn ceiling. "You have your speech ready?"

She heaves a sigh. "Mostly. I want to talk to my cousin before I finalize everything. There should be plenty of time after we get there tomorrow."

"I'm here to help with all the set-up and stuff."

As am I.

Ags grins as she takes out her earrings and removes the excess of chains around her neck. "I appreciate it, both of you."

Missy, never one to be excluded, jumps onto the little vanity in front of Ags and gives a little yowl.

"Yes." Ags gives Missy scratches behind her ear. "You're a big help too."

I sit up a bit, looking over at my little black cat. "She seems..."

"Smarter?"

"Yeah, more intelligent since everything with Skia."

You're welcome.

I shake my head with half a chuckle as Skia darts around the shadows in the room to get near the vanity as well. Missy jumps down, and Skia clings to her back as she snakes under Ags' bed.

Ags meets my gaze. "She is, though. It's a little eerie."

At this, I let out a snort. "I mean, she was possessed by a demon. It doesn't get much eerier than that, does it?"

"Fair point," Ags cackles.

She finishes removing her plethora of make-up and rubs some sort of eucalyptus smelling lotion on her face. We turn down the lights so Skia and Missy can join us on my bed, and the four of us settle in for an episode of New Girl before bed. We were bingeing Supernatural for a little bit, but I got tired of the constant comments about what they got wrong about demons.

Missy is asleep before the episode ends. Skia curls up beside her, their textures the only way to distinguish where one ends and the other begins.

Ags goes to her bed and turns out the light, leaving only a beam of moonlight coming through the thin curtains of the window. She shifts for a few minutes before settling, and soon her steady, deep breathing tells me she's asleep.

I roll onto my side, absentmindedly stroking Missy a few times. I think back to a year ago, cooped up in my apartment with such limited human contact that I almost thought I was a ghost a few times. Missy was my only companion for a long time. As hard as Ags tried to get me out of my shell, out of my own head, I wasn't ready.

Not until Skia came along.

I smile as the little shadow shifts. A low hissing murmur fills the room as they talk in their sleep.

The wedding will be fun. An opportunity to meet some new people and get dressed up. It took me forever to pick out the gray suit I brought. It's a little drab for this kind of wedding—so said Ags at the store—but I have a rainbow swirl pocket square and tie to spruce it up.

A flash of excitement burns through my chest. I haven't worn anything fancy in years, and the last time it wasn't exactly a set of clothes I was comfortable in.

I fade to sleep thinking of silly dances, champagne, and wedding cake.

Five

A crash of glass wakes me, but I can't move. Fear grips my chest, my stomach, and my heart. My eyes are open, but they are the only part of my body I can control. The only part obeying my commands.

The realization that it is still night, that moonlight is what pours in from the broken window just within my vision, scares me even more.

Someone broke in.

I strain every fiber of my being as a form moves toward me through the dark. I manage a grunt, my vocal cords finally uttering a fraction of the screams and curses going through my mind.

Hands—leather gloves imprinted with small symbols that shine with a silver glow in the moonlight—reach toward me.

No. Not toward *me*. My gaze, which I hope is showing my fury rather than my fear, follows the figure as they reach beside me and come away with a soft black shadow tight in their grasp.

Tiny red eyes glint for a brief second. They meet mine. Betrayal, fear, pain, all clear as day on the not-quite-a-face of my friend.

I can't explain. Can't speak beyond another furious grunt as the figure clutching Skia backs toward the window. Unintelligible words are exchanged. Not with my friend. With someone outside.

Another glint of light shows some kind of cage. Metal, gold maybe, though it's impossible to tell from my prone position. I finally hear Skia, a faint sound in the back of my head, barely audible.

Demi? What's going—

Skia's soft hiss fades out and a retching, aching fury slams through my chest. I move. The muscles in my back shift. My fingers twitch.

I rise a few inches off the pillow, teeth gritted with effort.

The figure at the window turns to me, their hood too deep to make out any features. They raise their hand and snap their fingers.

Everything goes dark.

I come to with a jolt. Frantically flailing every limb to make sure they work; I practically fall out of bed. Sweat drenches me. Fury radiates through my still foggy head.

"Demi?"

I spin, whipping blankets off of me. Ags is just sitting up, blinking blearily and frowning in confusion.

"I had the strangest dream..."

A gust of cool air cuts off her words, and the two of us turn to the window. The broken window with a faint slip of moonlight glinting on shattered glass.

"Skia."

My voice trembles. I lunge from the bed, sprinting to the pair of jeans I slung over the back of a chair before going to sleep. I tug them on, dragging a sweater over my head as I try to shake through my gut-clenching fear and think.

Broken glass crunches underneath my thick socks.

"Demi," Ags says as she scrambles from her bed as well. "Careful."

I nod without looking at her and dust glass off the soles of my feet before pulling on my boots. A shard nicks my hand, but I barely notice. "What was that?" I ask, my tone not as sturdy as I'd like. "Why couldn't we move?"

"I thought..." Ags winces. She's moving almost as fast as I am, tugging on a cardigan and her shoes. "I thought it was a dream."

"Not a dream," I grunt. "Skia is gone."

I hesitate, a thought making my blood run cold.

"Missy?"

Ags blanches. She turns around the room and calls out for the cat as well. "Missy, come out sweetie."

Nothing moves. I blink back tears. "Why would someone take them? How long were we asleep again after—"

"Not long," Ags interrupts, shaking her head. She strides toward the door.

"How do you know?"

She points to an old-fashioned clock on the wall across from the window. "That's about all I could see from where I was. It's only been half an hour."

Relief hits me and is immediately doubled by a yowling from the open window.

I hurry toward the panes of broken glass. "Missy."

I expect her to leap into my arms, or at least tread carefully back into the room. Instead, she paces along the ground, glares those yellow eyes up at me, and yowls again.

Ags follows me to the window. She meets my eye. "Maybe she..."

"Knows where they took Skia, yeah."

I rush away from the window to snatch the keys off the dresser.

"What are we going to—"

"Get Skia back," I snap, my voice harsher than I mean it to be. I look at Ags, suck in a breath, and try again. "We're going to get Skia back."

The understanding shining through her eyes is part of why I value her friendship so much. She nods.

I look at my cat. "We're going through the door. Meet you in a second."

I swear Missy rolls her eyes, but I'm in too much of a hurry to think about that very hard. Within a minute, Ags and I are standing outside the window of our room. A brief concern about how much that's going to cost to replace plays through my mind—a reprieve from the worry eating through me about what is happening to Skia.

Missy darts forward as we arrive, rubs against my shin for half a second, and then scampers into the darkness.

“Good thing I charged my phone,” Ags mutters. She pulls up her flashlight app and the two of us hurry into the night after a very small, very black cat.

Six

We move through tall grass for a while. The cuffs of my pants grow damp. It must be early morning with the amount of dew on the ground and the soft gray light edging the horizon.

There is something reassuring in following Missy. She does not amble. She has purpose, a destination she's leading us to. Worry still gnaws at me as the sun gets closer to rising.

If the monsters who took Skia from us are outside when the sun comes up...

"How much further do you think?" Ags' voice is a comforting reprieve from my own thoughts.

I'm about to respond when Missy shoots out of the brush. We follow her onto an empty sidewalk and street. My eyes widen.

"Weren't we just here?"

Ags nods. "Main street. This is so strange."

I follow her gaze to a building a few yards down the road. Missy moves towards it, creeping with her front half close to the ground as though she's on the hunt. Even in the dim light, the red and white paint is visible.

"Is that the barn?"

I glance back the way we came and shake my head. Our hostel is only a few blocks away.

Missy pauses. She looks back at us, and her yellow eyes narrow.

"Coming," I whisper.

She waits for us to reach her, then paws my ankle and leads the way closer to the barn. Voices sound from inside, muffled and low but audible with how quiet the street is.

We crouch and move along the side of the barn as silently as possible.

There are wide windows at the top. They likely lead to the hay loft. The rear side of the building—our side—has a massive sliding door, but we have no idea what's inside. Or if the door is locked or barred.

Ags points up and mouths, "Window?"

I frown, chest tight with unease. A ladder. We need a ladder.

A hiss draws my attention. Missy sits a few yards away behind the next-door building. Her paw rests on a rusty-looking ladder.

I hurry to her. "You're getting creepy, you know that?" I whisper.

She says nothing as I heft the ladder. Of course, because she's a cat.

I shake my head a little. Missy's super-cat intelligence is something to think about another time.

I return to Ags, who has been leaning with her ear against the wall to the barn.

"They definitely have Skia in there," she practically breathes. She backs away, taking a scrunchy from her wrist and tying her long dark hair into a bun.

"This is going to make some kind of noise." I jerk my head at the ladder. "But we *need* to get in there and see what's going on."

Ags nods, chewing on her bottom lip. "I'll go to the street. Slam something? Maybe break a window?"

I swallow. That doesn't feel like enough yet also seems like too much. "I have another idea."

I set the ladder down and take off my sweater. With quick movements I tie the fabric around one of the top ends of the ladder. A bit of cloth snags on the cut on my hand and pulls. I grit my teeth as the skin opens more, blood oozing out. I wipe it on my pants.

Ags, seeing my intention with the ladder, quickly pulls off her cardigan and hands it over. I muffle the other side.

It's our luck the high window is already open. Something tells me they don't bother closing it unless there is bad weather, which also makes me worried there will be a bunch of sleeping birds in the too-clean hay up there.

Not that we have much of a choice.

Ags holds one side of the ladder, and I clench my fingers around the other. Sweating with effort and tension, we bring it down gently on the window ledge. There is a soft thump, barely louder than dropping rolled up socks onto carpet.

I take another moment to appreciate Agatha. She's stout and strong, a fair contrast to my thin frame. Without her help easing the top of the ladder down, I'd have made a ton of noise.

I hold my breath for a few seconds, listening hard. Ags' eyes are as wide as mine, fixed on the wood panels in front of us as though she'll be able to hear them if she concentrates hard enough.

My heart continues to thunder, but there is no more waiting. I crouch and pat my shoulder. Missy takes a deep breath, then launches onto her usual perch. With her tail curled around the back of my neck, I begin to climb.

I don't understand the confusion. You're meant to be intelligent creatures, yet my words are lost in the mundane delusion and ineptitude you possess.

I never imagined the scathing sound of pissed-off Skia would be so comforting.

Ags and I crouch at the edge of the hay loft. We crawled, staying low and grateful for the lack of creaking wood beneath us as we moved slowly toward the sounds of voices.

Four cloaked figures stand beneath us. They're surrounding a golden cage, set upon the center of the not-pentagram Skia and I noticed yesterday. A ton of candles have me itching to call the fire department, and the strong scent of rotten meat hangs in the air.

That won't be good for the tours.

My muscles tense at the response from the people below us.

"You're in our possession now, demon." One of the figures whips back their hood, and Ags practically vibrates with anger beside me.

It's the woman from the coffee shop, the barista who claimed to be a witch. Well, I guess she is a witch, given the set-up downstairs.

Her hair is down, dark curls falling around her face. Her expression is obscured from our vantage point, but I can picture the scornful look that probably accompanies her tone.

Possession? Skia laughs, the sound sending a chill up my spine. *You know nothing of possession. You're children, all of you. Playing at things you don't understand.*

A chuckle goes through the group.

"Oh, we understand." Another hood comes down, revealing a blonde woman with twin braids and heavy make-up. Sort of a preppy version of Wednesday Adams. "You're a demon. You have power beyond measure. Power mankind can only dream of."

I cock my head, an incredulous squint in my eye as I recall the way Nexus almost killed us in my apartment. Skia certainly has power. They stopped a handful of assholes jumping me in an alley. But compared to a gatekeeper from hell, they aren't exactly high up on the food chain.

The woman continues. "Power *we* want."

Skia gives an unmistakable hissing snort. They respond, the words fading into the back of my mind as a plan grows in my mind.

I pull out my phone, make sure it's on silent, and gesture for Ags to do the same. There is no danger of being overheard if we are texting each other.

Missy brushes against my leg, rubbing her head into my arm as though telling me I need to get on with it. I give a few reassuring scratches behind her ear and return to sending the plan to Ags.

Seven

"You *will* grant us your power."

The conversation between Skia and the four witches has been going on at least five minutes now. It's clear these women didn't have an entire plan formulated before they took my demon friend.

I am curious why Skia hasn't simply slid through the golden wires of the cage surrounding them, but there must be some reason. Possibly something to do with why they didn't melt out of the gloved hand that took them in the first place.

The increasing strain of Skia's voice tells me they aren't staying to play some twisted game to teach the witches a lesson.

What part of I can't use my demonic abilities *are you struggling to understand?* they hiss with growing frustration.

The blonde witch, who appears to be leading the group, snarls. "We captured you. According to the texts—"

What texts? Skia demands. *Words written by humans? They mean nothing.*

I glance at the window behind me. Ags is gone, headed to the car we left in front of our hostel. I'd thought about trying to get further up the coast yesterday, but now I'm glad we stayed in Salem. Though, maybe if we'd left town, these witches wouldn't have stolen Skia.

"If you can't give us what we want, you'll have to contact someone who can."

... What?

My chest tightens at the fear in Skia's tone.

"Yeah," another witch, with a flaming red and orange pixie cut, says. "You do look pretty small. We want something more."

I'm not sure what you mean.

The polite way Skia hisses across the minds of everyone here is scarier than when they are angry. I shift, moving across the hayloft for a better view of the golden cage my friend is trapped in.

"You have a way to contact hell."

It isn't stated like a question, but Skia's silence seems to irritate the witches. One steps forward with a small black object in their hand.

My spine tingles with apprehension. I suck in a breath as the woman presses the object through the bars of Skia's cage.

It's a taser.

I have to bite back the shriek of rage that wants to leap from my throat as an electric charge goes through the cage. Skia's shadow form morphs and mutates, spasms of darkness burning from the direct light of the electricity and the pain of the shock itself. The acrid stench of sulfur and melted plastic fills the space.

I duck down, clenching my hand into a fist. Blood from my small cut stains my fingers.

"You have a way to contact hell," the leader says in a callous, apathetic voice. "You can bring Satan here so we might make a deal."

I don't know how she speaks through the soft whimpering coming from Skia. Anger spikes like daggers in my heart and head.

Missy trembles beside me. Her back is arched, every hair on end, her eyes nearly slits.

The whimpering turns to panting breaths and then eases to Skia's regular voice. I poke my head back up. Skia is back to the lumpy shadow form, slightly smaller but no longer actually smoking.

You want me to contact Satan? The incredulity in Skia's tone worries me. I fear what these assholes will do when faced with Skia's rare brand of humor. *I'm... I'm a sneeze demon, you imbeciles. I've never met the Fallen Angel.*

There are noises of protest.

Skia cuts across them with a louder, more powerful intrusion into everyone's minds. *I am of the lowest rank of demon known to hell. I have existed for three thousand years and am considered a* child *by those who serve Lucifer. I barely have one name; he has a thousand.*

"But surely you can—"

You are asking an ant to speak to an elephant. A pebble to move the ocean. A mail boy to demand a consult with the CEO!

I stifle a snort at the last one. Something tells me my little shadow friend has been watching office dramas while I do classwork with my noise-canceling headphones on.

The cluster of witches finally seems to get what Skia has been saying. They step away, circling together and muttering in low voices. I know from experience how good Skia's lack-of-ears are.

I take advantage of the witches being distracted and move along the edge of the loft toward the ladder on the side. A plank of wood moans beneath my foot. I freeze, eyes wide as the chatter below halts.

How long has Ags been gone now?

"Who's there?" a voice calls up.

I wince, a shiver going up my spine as a sense of defeat sets in. Missy brushes past my leg, hurrying behind a crate and out of sight.

I try not to breathe.

A rush of air, hot and heavy and stinking of sage, swirls around me. The breath in my lungs eases out between my lips without my permission. I feel hollow. Empty. I cannot draw a fresh breath.

My hands clench and unclench. I take a few staggering steps toward the edge of the loft. My vision begins to blur and fear sets in.

Stop.

Skia's hiss is a desperate, angry sound.

The spell breaks. I can breathe again, though pain still lingers in my chest.

"Come down." I recognize the blonde's voice.

"Yes," one of the others says. "Come down so we can see you before we kill you."

I swallow. My not-cut palm rubs small circles over the center of my chest, trying to send away the thick hurt. "All right," I call. "I'm coming down."

Descending the ladder with my back to the witches is *not* ideal. But I do it. When I turn at the bottom, a flush fills my cheeks. The heat of anger, embarrassment, and fear paints my face red.

I'm only a few yards from the witches, the sigil, and Skia. Up close, their little black form is trembling.

"Are you okay?" I ask them directly, ignoring the cloaked women. Two of them stay near my friend. The other two hold different artifacts Ags could probably identify. The only one I recognize is the smoking bundle of sage.

Good to know they require items for their spells. The thought of someone being able to pull the air from my lungs like that any time they want is terrifying.

Skia snorts. A little plume of shadow dissipates above them. *Not nearly. These Morgana wannabees have been using magic, Demi.*

"I know." I take a step toward them, but the witches holding spell ingredients close in between us, blocking my path.

"Of course, we have." The tallest of the witches, a pale woman with straight black hair, removes her hood. She gives me half of a cursory glance, before facing Skia. "You are a powerful being. Pretending otherwise is a lie."

I swallow. The two witches who cast a spell on me—one of whom is the barista—keep their gazes trained on me. The others ignore me.

"They can't use their power," I cut in as the blonde opens her mouth again. "It's too dangerous."

"Ahh, so it has used power before?"

My lip curls. "*They* have, yes. And were nearly dragged back to hell for it."

To my horror, the witches light up with excitement. The blonde grins, glancing at her companions before crouching beside Skia.

"Excellent. You use some power, and we get a gate to hell."

Eight

"That's a really bad idea." Fear runs like beads of ice through my veins.

"Why?" The witch doesn't look my way.

Her fellows seem to have lost interest in me as well. Some of my pride suffers at the thought that they don't see me as any level of threat at all.

I answer her question anyway. "You have no idea what kind of forces you're dealing with. The *thing* that came to collect them last time nearly killed us. It won't have any interest in making deals with you."

"Maybe not before." The barista places her items on the side of a tractor. She flexes her hands.

My eyes widen at how dark her veins are. What should be pale blue lines just under her flesh are dark blue. They protrude from the skin, like miniature ridged mountains.

She meets my gaze, a wicked smile splitting her lips. "Things are different. There was a shift."

The lust for power in her eyes makes me wish I'd brought some sort of weapon. Who knows what would work against these people? But anything in my hand right now would make me feel less helpless.

"A vibration of power," the blonde says. She stands, briefly caressing the golden cage.

Skia flinches away from her fingers.

"Surely you felt it?" The pale witch raises an eyebrow. Her voice is ghostly and ethereal. The greed behind her words is unsettling.

"I don't know what you're talking about," I mutter. My mind whirls. These women are crazy. Clinically insane with strange magic to back up their disturbing plans. They need a medical facility. Therapy. Something.

Ags has to have been gone long enough by now. But without me to text her which plan to go with...

I take half a step closer to Skia. At the very least, maybe I can smash the cage. If Skia is free they can get outside, get to Ags. Get safe.

Almost as though they can hear my thoughts, a pair of little red eyes fix on me. Skia speaks, and though it's not *technically* using their demonic power they do use some of their own dwindling energy to make sure I'm the only one who can hear them.

You have to get out of here, Demi. They're dangerous. I don't want them to hurt you.

At the same time, three of the witches encroach upon me.

"You had to feel it."

"The change in the air."

"Impossible became possible."

"Hypothetical became real."

Their voices are hypnotic and disturbed. Only the blonde remains quiet, watching me. I meet her eye, choosing not to look at the ones closing in on me even though every instinct tells me to keep my attention on them.

"Why do this?" My voice is steady. I think my anger has hit a threshold beyond fear. "You clearly have magic. Do you really need more?"

"There is never enough." The low tone of her voice, the glint in her eye, and the determination in the set of her jaw pull a touch of pity from me.

"That sounds like a sad way to live."

The witches pounce.

Two grab my arms. I wrench away from their grasps, but the third uses that damn magic again. It's not as strong—maybe because only one is doing it. But I still choke on the air in my throat.

I grit my teeth and swing my clenched fist. My knuckles impact the barista's cheek. She gasps, fury and disbelief etched across her face.

I shake my stinging hand, a few drops of blood darkening the hay beneath my feet. My act of rebellion infuriates them; the two not holding the spell grab me again, their fingers gripping like talons against my skin.

The lack of oxygen takes the fight out of me. At least for now.

I focus on dragging air into my lungs, doubled over as my vision starts going dark again. It's like breathing through a thin straw.

Vaguely, as though across a crowded room, I catch the blonde witch's words. She directs them at Skia.

"Give us what we want, demon. Or your friend dies."

Please. Let them go. I'll... The strain in Skia's voice hurts more than the lack of oxygen. *I'll do it. I'll use my power. Just let them go.*

The air returns to me, and I stagger forward at the sudden full breath in my chest. I stare at Skia. Memories flash through my mind. The fear in their voice when we faced Nexus. Their willingness to sacrifice themselves back then as well, when we'd barely known each other. When my kindness was an alien concept to them.

The thought of Skia going back to a place where kindness is weakness, friendship is foolishness, and love is nonexistent fills me with an entirely different kind of sadness.

"Skia..." I murmur, meeting that red gaze.

"We will release them when a gate opens. No sooner. Your kind is devious. We are not fools."

A scoff dies in my throat as a new sound catches my attention. The witches notice as well. The blonde holds up a hand, looking from Skia to the barn door.

A rushing sound comes from outside. Wind, roaring and whipping though no part of the building shakes. Moaning, deep and guttural. Hissing, sharper than Skia's with occasional foreign words making their way through the noise.

"Well done." The blonde grins down at Skia. She looks to the barista witch. "Go; see if there is a way through."

With the witches' attention on the door they don't notice Missy prowling toward Skia's cage. Skia, for their part, doesn't correct the witch. I wonder how far away Ags parked. If the soundtrack she found will have something to give us away, or if it will loop and they'll figure it out.

Then again, the second the barista witch sees a parked car, windows rolled down, blasting haunted sounds found on YouTube, the jig is up.

Which means we need to move fast.

Nine

I move backwards, slow steps as the witches approach the barn door with all the greed of a Wall Street bro glinting in their eyes. We—Missy and I—need to get Skia out of that cage, get to a door, and get to Ags. The car will be ready to go, I hope.

The witches don't have a way to track us, I hope.

They won't follow us all the way to the wedding, I hope.

There is too much hope in this plan and not nearly enough guarantee.

Missy has claws out scratching at the ground. The sigil. She's disrupting the paint. Smart kitty.

I get a few feet from Skia when the blonde witch notices me.

"Stop," she snaps. But she moved toward the barn door, too. She's a few feet away.

I lunge.

My fingers latch around the thin metal of the golden cage, and I heft it. Knowing the force won't—shouldn't—hurt Skia, I hurl the thing as hard as I can.

Golden lines crack and splinter as the cage slams into concrete.

It breaks apart at the same time that the sounds from outside stop. The barista bursts back through the door, fury etches across her face.

"It was a trick," she spits.

But the blonde already knows this. She works her fingers, twisting her hands and muttering.

The sigil on the ground lights up. Red glows across the lines. Missy yowls and darts back. I frantically look from the sigil beneath my feet to the witch. She gives a wicked grin. My heart takes up an irregular beat. The blood in my veins warms to an uncomfortable level.

The sigil sputters. The red light hits scratch marks through the paint and falters. With a sound like a sputtering teapot removed from the stove, the paint returns to black.

The grin drops from the witch's face. Her lips twist into a furious scowl. "You can't keep this kind of power all to yourself."

I wince as she raises her hands again.

A familiar voice calls from behind me, at the back of the barn. "Only your kind tries to keep power to yourself. The rest of us share."

A flash of relief is quickly followed by worry as the witches turn their focus on Ags. My wiccan friend steps from the shadows. Her hands are raised, fingers decked with rings and some sort of pattern inked onto her palms with what looks like sharpie.

"Your greed will be your downfall. Those of us who understand and value community will only continue to grow."

The blonde woman scoffs. "*Strigas*," she hollers, calling the other witches to her side.

They hurry forward, pulling items from their cloaks and casting as one.

Fear clutches my chest. We need to run.

I look to the shattered cage, but there is no sign of Skia. Good, they got out.

Missy is moving toward Ags. I dart toward her, scooping as I go and shifting her in my arms until she gets in a sturdy position on my shoulder. When I reach Ags' side the air is already sparking with whatever dark magic the witches are setting into motion.

"We have to—" My voice fails me. I double over. Every exposed bit of flesh feels as though it's being burned.

Agatha keeps her gaze on the witches. "Take hold of my arm."

I do as she says. The burning eases. Not gone but lessened by whatever protective magic Ags has.

"What are we going to do?" I mutter.

My plan went as far as run-out-the-door. If they hadn't been torturing Skia, maybe I would have had time to come up with something better. As it is, I'm worried my little friend won't have enough shadow left to make it to the car without protection from the sun.

"Step back, slowly."

Ags' voice is already strained. Sweat beads along her forehead, and she's swaying slightly. The air warps around us, those little sparks unable to fully penetrate the field of goodness Ags gives off.

"You won't make it to the door." The blonde witch stops her chanting to taunt us. Flanking her, the others keep it up, their whole focus on the spell. "We're going to kill you, find your demon friend, and force it to give us what we want. You shouldn't have gotten involved."

But that's what friends do.

Skia's voice, distorted and deep, sounds from above, and everyone looks up. A shadow of darkness sits tucked into the corner of a rafter, red eyes glowing down at the witches.

Realization slams into me as my demonic friend drifts away from their perch. I turn, grabbing Ags by the shoulder and forcing her around. With our backs to the witches, we can't see exactly what Skia does. But the screams conjure enough to the imagination that I'm glad I'm not watching.

I walk us forward, Ags leaning on me hard as we make our way to the rear door. The screams stop after a few seconds. I don't let us look back.

We get through the door. Light pours over us. The sun has risen.

"Go," I say, leaning in so Missy can get to Ags' shoulder. "Get to the car. We'll be right there."

"Demi—"

"Go."

Ags, leaning hard on the exterior wall of the barn, heeds my words.

I watch her go, blinking in the bright light. Then I take a deep breath, square my shoulders, and hurry back into the barn.

Ten

The center of the barn is no longer concrete. Red and orange molten edges ring an eight-foot-wide pit of darkness that is worse than any sort of gate to hell my imagination could have created. The witches stand at the four cardinal directions.

Floating above the black is a shadow that is far too small. Skia seems to have shrunk by half with the use of their power. They're barely bigger than Missy's head.

I don't think they're the one who opened the pit.

Their effect on the witches is evident in the black oozing from the women's eyes, ears, and noses. They stand frozen, eyes wide with horror either at what Skia did or the consequences of demonic power.

There is barely time to contemplate which.

Spindly legs, some scaled, some coated in peach fuzz, and some spiked, reach up through the opening.

I take a few steps back, my heartbeat thundering in my ears.

The blonde witch vibrates where she stands. With a grunt of effort that sends another rush of black ooze from her nostrils, she breaks free of Skia's power.

"Great forces of darkness," she calls, her eyes alight with excitement. "We come to you for a deal. Our abilities have grown great, but we know there is much, much more. Let the Coven of Striga serve you."

My stomach roils at the stench of sulfur emanating from the pit. Smoke seeps out, tendrils of it wrapping around the legs of the witches on all four sides.

"WE NEED NOTHING FROM YOU."

Every instinct in me flinches at the voice coming from below.

A long strand of smoke reaches toward Skia.

"BUT IF YOU WOULD GIVE YOUR SOULS SO WILLINGLY..."

I suck in a breath through pursed lips. "This is nuts." I step back again, giving myself room for the insanity I'm about to attempt.

The strands of black tighten around the witches' legs.

I grit my teeth and sprint straight toward the pit.

The acrid air stings my lungs. I heave thick breaths, fear pushed aside as that strand reaching for Skia makes contact with my shadowy friend.

My foot reaches the edge. I leap.

Heat pummels my skin. I don't look down. Don't want to see what is in that hellish chasm. My sight is set on Skia. I reach, scooping like I've done so many times these past few months that Skia has been part of our little family.

Barely any weight, but enough to reassure me that I have them, settles in my arms.

We slam to the ground on the far side of the pit. I roll, pain thudding through my shoulder and hip on the side where I landed.

With Skia still firmly clenched in my arms, I dash the short distance to the door and race into the waiting sunlight.

"What about Nexus?" Ags asks anxiously. Her hair is a frizzy mess from how many times she's run her ringed hands through it. She shoots a glance behind us.

I exhale and look in the rearview mirror. We've left Salem behind. The highway is ahead, the Atlantic Ocean to our right as we make our way north. Should be at the wedding venue by late afternoon. Not as early as planned, but with plenty of time to help set up before tomorrow.

A chuckle escapes me. A mix of incredulity that I'm even thinking about the wedding right now, and a bit of the leftover fear that needs a way out of my body.

"What?" Ags demands.

I shake my head, concentrating back on the road. "I don't think we need to worry about that right now. Whatever was coming out of that pit didn't look like Nexus."

Most demons have been gone from this plane for a long time. I doubt Nexus, or any others who may emerge to find me, can track us at this speed.

I glance at the odometer with a raised eyebrow. "Seventy?"

Horse and carriage, Demi. That is what my kind is used to.

"I guess that makes sense," Ags says, a bit of relief in her tone. She strokes Missy, currently settled comfortably in her lap.

"And you, pretty little miss." Ags shoots me a glance. "I'm very curious about exactly how intelligent she is now."

I nod at the same time that Missy lets out a little mew. "Don't worry, Missy. We won't have you doing tricks for treats. We know you're not a dog."

The joke is offset by a satisfied sounding purr. Ags lets out a tight chuckle.

I adjust the sweater draped over my legs and take a peek at Skia. They're huddled below, out of the way of the car pedals but still brushing against my calves. Concern stirs in my stomach at how small they are after everything that happened.

Then again, we haven't eaten anything. I tighten my grip on the steering wheel.

"I want to go a few more hours before we stop to eat, but we should get food soon."

Agreed, Skia hisses. *My form has shrunk considerably. A bowl of fries. Or perhaps a brownie. Ice cream...*

They continue on like that for a while. Ags laughs, the tension in her shoulders loosening at Skia's lack of worry.

I can't quite get past the nerves bunched in my gut. There are too many unanswered questions. And that voice, deep and terrifying and unworldly, still rings through my ears when the car gets too quiet.

Part of me wants to know what became of those witches. Part of me never wants to find out. And another part of me is viciously glad for whatever horrible fate awaits them. They deserve it for hurting Skia.

Agatha's cousin, Stacey, isn't bothered at all by our lateness. She and her partner, an ex-Navy man the size of a tree trunk, are all laughs and smiles. I'm reluctant to risk anyone seeing Skia, but that becomes a non-issue when the soon-to-be newlyweds show us a pair of adjoined rooms at the cottage-style hotel where the wedding is going to happen.

We unpack, and I leave Skia in the room with Missy. The curtains are drawn, the lights are off, a box of pizza is open on the bed, and New Girl is playing on my laptop.

Set up is fun, even with my bruised shoulder and the bandage on my hand. These are the kind of people who enjoy the wanderlust, whimsical side of life. We line the ceremony arch with moss, mushrooms, fairy lights, and ceramic butterfly wings. The weather should hold, so setting out the benches and decorative flowers early isn't an issue.

Stacey and Tyler don't even mind when I excuse myself as the night-before party gets going.

I can't stand the thought of being away from Skia longer than necessary. And I'm utterly exhausted.

I gobble down the last slice of cold pizza when I return to the room, give Missy a few scritches behind her ear, and lay down next to Skia.

In the darkness, only their glowing red eyes are visible.

What is wrong, Demi?

I huff out a laugh. "I mean, this morning wasn't exactly my idea of a fun stop on a road trip."

They are silent for a minute.

I shift, leaning on my elbow to look at them. "They hurt you."

They did.

"I'm sorry."

Nothing that happened this morning was your fault, Demi. Except our escape. If you hadn't done what you did, I'd be a minuscule ball of darkness, fading away in that cage. Or I'd be sucked back to that infernal place. They shudder.

"I wouldn't let that happen." My voice is strained; the knowledge that it's not as simple as that is very present in my mind.

Skia clearly thinks the same, as a low hissing laugh reverberates through my head. After a moment the laughter ceases. *It was... unsettling to see magic of that nature in the world again.*

"Again?"

It was prevalent at one time. Long, long ago. Before I was allowed on this plane the first time.

I sit with that for some time. "Is there anything we can do about it? Are we safe now those witches are gone?"

Skia snorts. *The Coven of Striga? A rather obvious name, by the way. And no. I don't believe this business of demonic power available to humans is done.*

I nod, weariness dragging at me. This feels too big for the amount of energy left in my body. I lay my head back on the pillow. "Sounds like a tomorrow problem."

Of course. There certainly isn't anything to be done about it tonight.

My voice is muffled as I turn and cradle the pillow under my head. "We're safe though, right? No more paralysis in the dead of night? No pits to hell?"

We're safe, Demi. I'm keeping my senses active now I know what threats lurk on this plane. That pit closed up not long after we got away.

"You can know that?" Sleepiness pulls my eyes closed.

I can know that. It will mean consuming more of your scones to keep up my energy. But there are a handful of things I can do without calling on the forces of hell.

"Good, good."

Skia's shadowy shape, a little heavier after downing nearly a whole pizza, settles into the crook of my arm, pressed against me like a comfort plushy. On the other side, Missy does the same.

The wedding is gorgeous. Stacey is a vision in her lacey gown, violet and white flowers woven through the train and her hair. Tyler is in his military uniform, a stark contrast to the rest of the union, but a dashing visage all the same.

I look pretty dang good myself. This is the first time I've ever felt comfortable at a wedding. Not forced into what my family thought was appropriate, but wearing something that makes me happy.

Agatha wears her signature black and purple. Ruffled sleeves hang low as she pulls forth the vows. Her voice carries to the back of the bench seating, clear and purposeful. It seems to move every attendee to sit a little straighter. Soft wind blows through the trees around us and, as the bride and groom exchange a kiss, a cascade of lavender colored petals descend over us all.

Where they came from is a question only I am asking, as none of the trees near us are flowering and no one threw them.

My lip twitches into a smile as Ags gently touches the newlyweds' shoulders before they head down the aisle.

A spark of gold lingers where her fingers landed, and my smile grows.

Book
Three
Spelling
Disaster

One

There is something lovely about a Saturday morning farmers market. Even if I do have to hide Skia in my oversized hoodie the whole time. They aren't the best at picking out eggs, but they somehow always know which cantaloupe is ripe.

It's a beautiful start to the day. Until I catch sight of a leather vest, spiked blond hair, and a pair of aviator sunglasses.

My cantaloupe cracks on the concrete.

The day takes a decided turn.

Run.

The instruction is unnecessary, but I heed Skia's frantic command and sprint down the side alley as fast as my legs can carry me—us. Skia is in the hood of my sweater, their favorite place to be and the only reason I'm wearing one when it's nearly ninety-three degrees outside.

A choice I regret as my arms pump at my sides, adrenaline replacing the fear in my blood.

Our farmers market treats are scattered across the sidewalk. A necessary sacrifice to maintain distance from the man pursuing us.

Footsteps pound the asphalt behind me: the heavy black boots of a man who looks like a mercenary straight out of an action movie as he gives chase.

A knife flies past me and thunks into the brick wall to my left. Too close.

"I told you," I huff, "not to... practice... outside of Agatha's."

Is now the time? Skia's voice in my head is more scared than I've heard it all summer.

We've been dodging Axel—a bounty hunter hired by hell—for over a month. The man caught our trail after Agatha used some harmless magic at a wedding ceremony. Turns out all magic is trackable, not just Skia's special brand of demonic power.

"Can't run forever," calls a distinct, winded Australian accent. I glance back and catch sight of the bounty hunter pulling another weapon from his belt.

I stuff my "I told you so" rant away for later and focus on the map in my head. I've lived in this city for years. I know these streets. The roads and alleys and shops that make up downtown are a maze for most.

For me, it's a jungle gym.

I zip left down a busy street, dart into a small corner store, and with a nod at the old Korean woman behind the counter, hurry through the building and out into a new alley. Then I double back the way we just came from, slowing at intersections to make sure Axel isn't waiting.

Lost him, Skia breathes, their voice just a whisper across the front of my mind.

I nod. "Get into the front pocket."

They obey. A shadow of black glides across my shoulder and down into the front pocket of my hoodie. I push the sleeves up past my elbows, breathing hard and making a mental note to never forget Skia's travel backpack again. It's hot.

I do another quick check to make sure a towering, black-leather clad man with multiple rune-inscribed knives and trinkets hasn't found us. Pretty sure we left him in the dust several blocks back, but few things would be worse than accidentally leading Axel to Agatha's Emporium.

After ensuring Skia has no whisps of smoke sticking out of my pockets—both for appearances and because they would burn away in the sun—I step onto a main thoroughfare full of people and begin an as-neutral-as-possible stroll to my friend's shop.

Why do you insist on participating in classes full of falsehoods?

I sigh and close my laptop. Free of the hoodie and enjoying the air-conditioned comfort of Agatha's Emporium, I'm a bit more relaxed.

There is also the plus of having warding sigils all over the place here. Nothing strong enough to attract attention, but according to Agatha and Skia the runes keep us somewhat invisible and allow Skia to use their own personal store of power without alerting Axel's tracking capabilities.

They mute the "disturbance of magical energy." Whatever that means.

"I want to know how different places and peoples think of stuff like this." I gesture vaguely at Skia sitting in the right bowl of an antique scale, Agatha behind the counter measuring ingredients into little containers, and Missy cocking her head at me with an appraising look I still haven't gotten used to.

Why? Humans know nothing.

"Hey," Agatha barks from her stool behind the counter. She gives Skia a squinty glare, her sparkling purple eyelids nearly closing. Her eyeliner is needle-sharp, hair pinned back in a messy bun while she works, and lips as vibrant red as ever.

Skia adjusts their words. *Next to nothing.*

Ags rolls her eyes, but her temper cools as Missy hops onto the countertop for pets.

I grin. My little black cat has been making a habit of emerging for snuggles whenever the late summer heat gets on any of our nerves. Or when a bounty hunter nearly catches us on accident because we wandered through the farmers market at the wrong time.

"The point isn't to take everything in these classes as gospel," I say with an exhale. I stretch and crack my neck. My shirt is still damp from sweat. "But if we want to travel, find more people with abilities like Ags, and learn more about what is going on with all this magic stuff, it'd be good to have an idea of what people already think."

Agatha nods, then looks to the front door. It's a Saturday, but summer has been slow for business. Things will likely pick up when autumn arrives.

"When do classes start?" she asks.

I grimace. "I can sign up in a week, then actual classes are another month out. But I'm thinking I should go back to all online."

A furrow mars her smooth bronze skin. "Why?"

It's my turn to glance toward the front of the shop. A sinking feeling makes my stomach clench.

The spring wedding Agatha officiated was beautiful. But the preceding danger to Skia, and the proceeding fear of being chased by a bounty hunter working for *hell*, was and is a lot on the nerves. I haven't gotten a good night of sleep since we left the east coast.

"Axel isn't going to stop hunting us," I murmur, not wanting to drop the mood. "Going to classes at the same time on consistent days of the week feels kinda dumb. He doesn't know what you look like." I give Ags a nod. "But my face is recognizable."

Even after the haircut, Skia agrees. Their little shadowy self bounces just enough to shift the scales.

At the counter, Missy mews. Ags scratches behind her ear with long nails.

"We'll figure something—" Agatha begins. But she's cut off by a little jingle from the front door.

Missy leaps from the counter, hurrying to the cushy armchair next to mine and pawing at the pillow. Skia darts to it, their shape conforming to the shadowy space made available. Missy curls up beside the pillow.

From more than a foot away it looks as though Skia is simply my cat's shadow.

I stand, worry caught in my throat even as I marvel at how ridiculously smart Missy has become.

The quickening of my pulse is steadied as Agatha's lips split into a smile.

"Welcome to Agatha's Emporium," she calls, striding around the counter and making toward the young blonde woman who has just entered the shop. "What can I do for you today?"

I follow Ags at a casual pace, curious about the hurried look of the woman who just pushed through the doors.

She appears to be in her early twenties with a high pony and wide green eyes. Both hands are in front of her chest, clutching something small in her fingers. She takes a deep breath.

"I need your help."

Two

"Start at the beginning."

I glance at Ags, then cross to the chair where Skia is still hiding behind the shadow of a pillow and perch on the edge. Missy rises and gracefully leaps to the floor.

Across from me, the blonde woman, Kate, sits straight-backed and tense on a footstool. Offers for her to take the remaining comfy chair were met with vehement head shaking.

Her hair is long, flowy, and curled with a gentle wave at the end of the ponytail. Her cheeks are still flushed, either from the heat outside or the hurry to get here. An old JanSport backpack dangles from her shoulder. She hasn't made any move to put it down.

Curiosity threatens to shoo away my manners because her hands are still tight to her chest, but I'm pretty sure I just saw something move between her fingers.

A whisper of suspicion stirs in my veins. A warning to remain alert around this woman. There was a time I'd ignore my instincts, call them paranoia, but not after everything my little family has been through these past few months.

Easy. Skia's murmurs in my head. *You're practically squishing me. Relax.*

I shift to the side, wishing I was able to respond in the same way. But speaking directly into people's heads is a demonic trait that cannot be learned.

They're right though. I'm on edge. I rest my hand on the cushion and a thin tendril of smoke curls around my pinky in a comforting gesture.

Agatha settles into the vacant chair, crossing her hands delicately in her lap and giving Kate a look that reminds me of every fortune-teller I've ever seen in a movie. Even her skirts are splayed out in a way that oozes mysticism.

Kate glances my way for a fraction of a second. I give a tight smile.

"It's all right." Ags' soothing voice seems to bring calm to the trembling woman. "This is a safe place. Tell us what happened."

Missy rubs against my shin, and I reach down to give her a pet. She sniffs the air.

"So, it was right after the semester ended." Kate speaks with urgency. She looks at Ags as she stumbles over her story. "My best friend got dumped, so she borrowed a book from my Nona and then came here wanting to get stuff for, like, a witchy girl's night or whatever. She got herbs and some chalk and candles and stuff."

Agatha nods.

I ignore the silent scoff that echoes in my head and adjust the pillow Skia is hiding behind.

Missy pads toward our guest, her little black nose in the air as though she's caught the scent of bacon.

"Well, they ended up getting back together so that didn't happen." Kate's strained expression slips into an angry frown. "But last week I found out my boyfriend, Trevor, was cheating on me with *two different girls* from our sociology class, and then when I confronted him, he said it was my fault for prioritizing school work over our relationship."

I grimace. Ags murmurs her condolences. Kate grits her teeth for a second, then shakes her head and sucks in a deep breath.

"Anyway, we had all the stuff from here, and the book, and three bottles of wine from a wedding we just went to and... It was supposed to just be for fun. I don't even believe in any of that junk. But then..." Her eyebrows draw together in a look of such desperation that a flash of pity surges through me. "It was an accident. And I don't know how to fix it..."

Missy turns her yellow eyes on me for a brief second, her whiskers twitching with mischief. She prances closer to Kate, tilting her head as she sniffs the woman's hands.

Kate lets out half a broken chuckle and smiles down at the cat.

Keeping her fingers together like a cage, Kate reveals what she's been holding onto this whole time. A small green and white lizard blinks out from between her palms.

Its tongue flicks out, licking its eyeball before it catches sight of Missy and begins scurrying frantically back and forth in Kate's hands.

I raise an eyebrow, confusion slowly melting into horror as, in my head, Skia says, *Oh my.*

Kate inhales, looking from me to Agatha with her brows pinched together in a desperate frown. "This is my ex."

Three

We barely have time to process when the lizard—Trevor—slips through Kate's fingers and shoots across the floor like a kid on a slip-and-slide.

"Missy, no!" I jump after the cat, but she's given chase.

The lizard scurries under a hutch displaying an assortment of crystal balls. Missy barrels toward it with all the intent of a predator cornering her prey.

"Do *not* break Agatha's things," I snap.

That seems to do it. Missy backpedals into a stop only an inch from the ornate wooden shelving unit. She narrows her yellow eyes at me and bares her teeth.

I sigh. "That's not a normal lizard, Missy. You can't chase it around."

She flicks her tail.

"Or eat it," I mutter as I get on all fours and duck my head to try and find the damn thing.

Sure enough, the green and white man-turned-reptile is cowering in the least accessible corner. I reach, but it scootches back even further. My shoulder can't get under the hutch.

I retreat, scoop Missy into my arms, and join Agatha and Kate at the check-out counter where my friend is trying to calm the newcomer.

"Let's start simple," Ags says. Only knowing her for years allows me to detect the tension in her steady voice. "Do you have this book you mentioned?"

Kate nods, her eyes red from rubbing away tears. With her hands now free, she takes off her backpack, unzips it, and dumps the contents onto the counter.

A half-burned candle, twigs of some kind of herb, a sandwich baggie of ash, and a thick book that looks older than the Presidency all pour out.

"This is everything," Kate says with a glance at the hutch. "Should we... do you have anything we can put him in while we talk?"

I give Missy ear scratches to try and pacify her. The usual purrs are replaced with a glowering look at me. I roll my eyes and turn my attention to Kate.

"Took a while to catch him the first time?"

"Yeah," she says with a grimace. "It's why I didn't get here right when you opened. I spent most of the morning trying to find him in my apartment."

Agatha meets my eye. "I think we know someone who could get him out of there." She digs around behind the counter and comes up with an old shoebox. "And I can poke some holes in this."

I huff out a breath. The past months have been spent keeping Skia hidden and safe. It feels abnormal to let a stranger see them.

Then again, this specific stranger turned her ex into a lizard last night. She's already in this weird world of magic. Whether she wants to be or not.

I've got it, Skia hisses.

Kate jolts, backing against the counter as her wide eyes search for the source of the voice that just echoed through her head. "Who... what—"

"So, this is Skia," I say in as soothing a voice as possible.

My shadowy friend slinks out from under the pillow and drifts to the ground. They move like a cloud on the wind, only faster. It's a bit unsettling to see the first few times, and I step in front of Kate so she doesn't feel like they're coming right at her.

"What..." She swallows and takes a deep breath before continuing. "What is it, exactly?"

Skia slides toward the hutch, glinting red eyes the only way to tell where their front is.

"They're a sneeze demon." I turn to her. "And they'll probably be able to get Trevor out from under the hutch."

"Right." Kate's voice is soft and high. After a few seconds of bewildered blinking, she straightens and turns to Agatha. "Do you think you can turn him back into an asshole?"

I snort.

Skia's haunting laugh dances through everyone's heads again.

Kate blanches but keeps her eyes on Agatha.

My friend gives a faltering smile. "I can look at all of this, but I don't want to promise anything. I've never—" She glances at me.

I move closer, setting Missy on the counter and looking at Kate. "Ags does defensive magic. All protection-type stuff. And even with that, we're still new to actual, practical magic."

Kate lets out a shaky exhale. "But you sell all of this."

I give a weak shrug. "Yeah, for people who want to practice wiccan stuff. For those wine and witchy nights."

"It's only recently that my magic has begun working in a more real sense," Ags murmurs. "But we've not... you're the first person who has come in like this."

Kate gestures vaguely around the shop. "But... none of it is supposed to be real, I—"

I cut her off as gently as possible. "This is new to us all."

Agatha and I exchange a brief look.

I continue, "Can you tell us exactly what you did?"

There is a pause in the conversation as Skia swoops out from under the hutch. The lizard is caught in a makeshift cage created with whisps of their smoke-like substance.

Where is the creature's prison?

Ags fights back a smile and takes off the lid to the shoe box. Skia deposits the lizard, and she quickly puts the lid back in place. Just before a little black paw darts towards it.

"Missy," Ags scolds.

The cat lets out a defeated yowl and slumps down onto the counter, her gaze trained onto the gray box.

Kate clears her throat and nods. "Right. So we found a page that looked good, drew some symbols on a sheet over the hardwood, and then drank a ton of wine and burned some candles. Then we watched Practical Magic, drank even more wine, and went to bed." She looks at her hands, desperate disbelief etched into her expression. "It wasn't supposed to actually *do* anything."

"How do you know that," I point at the box, "is Trevor?"

She rubs her temple. "He came over this morning to pick up some of his stuff and when he stepped on the sheet—"

He melted into a reptile.

As pale as she is, it's hard to tell if Kate is still affected by Skia's voice or if she's already used to it.

She nods again. "He was screaming, I was screaming, and then there was a freaking lizard scurrying around my apartment. None of my friends believed me that it's Trevor, but I watched it happen."

A delay on the spell. Skia's voice carries a thoughtful tone. *That suggests powerful magic.*

Kate swallows. With a nervous glance at the demon, she looks at Agatha. "Can you help me?"

Ags looks at me, her eyes wide with uncertainty. "I'm still not sure how you managed..."

The hesitation in her voice sends a pang of sadness through me. My friend likes having the answers. She likes knowing things and sharing that knowledge with others. Finding herself unable to help someone has to hurt.

I brush my fingers across the array of things Kate dumped on the counter. As I reach the book, Skia speaks again.

"You didn't get this here." They follow my movements, gliding over to the book in question and appraising it with glowing red eyes.

"No," Kate says. "It's my Nona's."

This has... far too much magic.

Worry stirs in my stomach at the tension in Skia's voice.

"Too much for the wards?" Ags asks. She reaches for her oversized purse.

It's very possible.

Agatha nods, exchanges a glance with me, and begins shoveling items into her bag.

I look at Kate. "Where *is* your Nona? We might need to go pay a visit."

Four

Getting to Kate's Nona's house sounds like it will be simple enough. She lives a couple of hours outside the city on a nonoperational ranch their family used to run. All we have to do is get to Agatha's car—a little junker she keeps parked in the multi-level garage on the corner–and make our way east.

Sounds simple.

Until Skia, perched on my shoulder as I pack up my things, says something that sinks a stone-like weight into my gut.

Agatha, is the front door locked?

We all turn as one.

Kate glances from the door to the rest of us, her eyes wide. "Do you guys know that dude?"

Standing on the other side of the tinted glass is Axel. His face is slightly obscured by the shelves between us and the window, but there is no mistaking the black pants, leather vest, and multitude of weapons on his belt. He moves slowly, taking in the storefronts.

"I did lock it, Skia," Agatha murmurs. She does up the last buckle on her purse and pats her shoulder.

Missy leaps from the counter to the spot in a graceful movement.

"But I don't imagine that will hold him for long." Ags hefts her purse and strides purposefully toward the back of the shop.

Kate looks at me and Skia. "So you *do* know that guy."

It's a long story, Skia says. *I'll happily explain... once we're well away from him.*

Kate raises an eyebrow, her gaze sliding from Skia's red eyes to my hazel ones.

I nod. "We really should go."

She snatches her backpack from the chair and hurries after me. We follow Agatha past the checkout counter, through a sparkly black curtain, and down a long narrow hallway.

I pull open the heavy exterior door that leads to the parking garage access walkway. Kate hurries through and, as I turn to follow her, the crash of breaking glass sounds behind me.

Faster, Skia urges. Their voice is not in my head alone, evidenced by Kate's shift from walking to jogging.

Further ahead, Missy has opted to run alongside Agatha rather than ride her shoulder in the rush to escape.

"Who the hell is that guy?" Kate demands, glancing back at me.

Who the hell, indeed.

Even with fear gripping me tight, I can't help a half-hearted chuckle.

"Bounty hunter," I say.

I catch up to her, jogging alongside as we take a sharp right and are spat out into a large parking garage. Shadows loom behind every column. Parked cars are both places to hide and places people—or demons—might be lurking.

"Bounty hunter?" Kate's incredulous tone echoes against the concrete walls and ceiling.

Shh.

I take a left, following Agatha's flowing skirts as she swishes rapidly through the cars to her beat-up tan Toyota Corolla.

"Yep," I say in a hushed voice as Agatha unlocks the car and we all pile in. "A bounty hunter. Hired by hell. There's an essence or aura or something that goes off when people use magic. From what we can tell, this guy has been tracking down those auras."

Ags turns the key, throws the Corolla in reverse, and pulls out of the parking spot.

Kate twists in the passenger seat, staring at me with a horrified expression. "What does he do when he finds them?"

"Great question." I take off my backpack and set it on the floor, then lean across the backseat to lock the door. "To be honest, we haven't been that keen to find out."

Skia lets out a laugh lightly tinged with fear. Then they stop. They shift on the seat, and for a moment, I think they're worried about the sunlight about to stream through the windows. I get my sweater ready for them to hide under but...

Demi.

Then I also realize what's missing.

“Wait!” I curse under my breath, leaning forward to glance at the front with little hope that I’ll find what I’m looking for.

Both women look back at me, bewildered.

I slap a hand to my forehead.

“We forgot the damn lizard.”

Five

This seems unwise.

I nod; Skia is correct. This is unwise.

Unwise but necessary. Because we have no clue what happens to magical stuff when Axel gets ahold of it, and as much of a jerk as Trevor sounds like, I don't think we should test the limits of hell's cruelty on the guy.

So, with Skia tucked into the large pocket of my sweatshirt—again—I press against the exterior front wall of Agatha's Emporium, preparing myself to run in and grab the shoebox containing a cheating ex-boyfriend.

Ags, Missy, and Kate wait in the car just around the corner. An SOS is all set in the message app on my phone, resting beside Skia in my pocket. The car is in drive, ready to race down the alley as soon as Skia's shadow tendrils push send.

But first we have to get the box.

I scoot along the side, my hood snagging on the bricks as I approach the shattered front door.

I cringe at the thought of Agatha having to pay for all of this. Glass is strewn across the pavement, and it doesn't sound as though Axel is being particularly careful with Agatha's delicate items.

He sounds like an elephant in a tea shop.

I push past the desire to correct my demon friend and step carefully through the jagged threshold.

Axel is somewhere near the back of the store, based on where all the noise is coming from.

Glass crunches under my shoes, but the sound is minimal compared to the clanging and cursing.

Careful. Skia's shadow head pokes out of my pocket.

I can't respond, but I have to believe the thundering of my pulse is audible to their demon senses. Of course I'm being careful.

I move through the shop quickly. The shelves help block me from view, but they also stop me from seeing exactly where Axel is. I step around the final obstacle and spot the shoebox. It sits in the center of the check-out counter.

Fully in the open.

Down the dark hall, the banging stops.

I grit my teeth, dart forward, and snatch the box.

"Well, well, well, look who finally showed themselves."

My breath catches, heart pounding as a massive hand—clad in a fingerless glove with little studs on the knuckles—pushes aside Agatha's sparkly curtain and a very large man steps into the main room of the store.

Axel's thick Australian drawl and his spiked dirty-blond hair threaten to be mildly humorous, but the multitude of daggers at his belt and the glinting, predatory look in his eye solidify the instinct to be afraid.

"Just picking up something. Feel free to continue the wreckage." I gesture at the shards of broken glass, shredded pieces of paper, and scatterings of dirt from many destroyed plants, without taking my eyes off the bounty hunter.

"You've been evading me for a while now." He steps forward, boots crunching the glass, gaze scanning me in a way that feels more like an airport x-ray than the usual creepy-guy eyeing. "Ahh," he says as he catches sight of my large hoodie pocket, "that's where you're hiding."

Less hiding, Skia says in both our heads. *More catching a ride.*

In my own head, they continue, *Demi, move slowly. Back us toward the door.*

I obey. Axel follows. His boots are loud on the ground, but a soft jingle also catches my attention. A small silver trinket hangs from a leather cord attached to his belt.

"Don't try anything stupid here, kid."

My lips twist in a grimace. "What exactly do you want with us?"

Keep going.

I take another few steps, slowly moving backward while I keep my eyes on Axel. This face to face has been coming for a while now. My grip is so tight I'm making little divots in the shoebox.

Don't let him get too close. Skia whispers through my head again.

"I wasn't planning to," I growl.

Axel, mouth open and about to answer my question, cocks his head. "Ahh. The two of you are having a private conversation? That's rude."

"Rude?" My incredulity momentarily steals my common sense. "Rude is tracking people across the country and destroying their livelihood."

A brief flush reddens the bounty hunter's cheeks as he glances around the store.

"Rude is snatching up magical things and doing who-knows-what with them."

Accepting a bounty from hell might be considered rude.

Axel snarls. "Stay outta my head, demon."

I step backward again. The busted door to the shop is only about ten feet from me now. The summer heat presses against my sweatshirt, fighting the air conditioning of Agatha's store.

"That *thing* doesn't belong here." Axel's hand moves to his side.

I swallow as he pulls a silver blade from its sheath and points the tip at my chest.

"Why not?" I demand. If I keep him talking maybe I can get through the door before he lunges. Then again, maybe I'll end up with a dagger in my back.

"It's unnatural," Axel's voice, the words themselves, grate against my nerves.

I shake my head and take another half step. All that's left between us and freedom is a rickety bookshelf that once held flower vases and candles. It's empty now, the shelves themselves barely more than splintered wood.

"What is? A demon?"

"All of it." He flips the blade in his hand. "The demon, the magic, you helping it... it's upsetting the balance. Which is why you gotta go, and that demon has to come with me."

I'm hitting the button, Skia says to me. *Keep him talking. Find out what they're paying him.*

"Why you?" I ask, unable to respond to Skia with anything besides pressing the box tighter to my chest. "Why didn't hell just keep sending demons?"

"And put even more of them on our plane?" He scoffs. "You don't get it. Any of it. What else would I expect from some Yank with no training in the mystic?"

Despite the absolute truth of his words, I'm offended.

Why are you stopping? Skia's tone is a mix of frightened and annoyed.

I skip over my frustration. "What is hell giving you to make it worth all this effort?"

Axel sneers. He flips the blade again, shifting his stance as though he's about to pounce.

"Your weight in gold, kid. Any last words?"

I hear something in the distance. The squeal of tires. The gurgle of a very old Toyota Corolla engine.

"Yeah." I heave a sigh and shake my head. "You're ruining Steve Irwin's accent for me."

I side-step and, with a grunt of effort, shove the bookshelf. Already off kilter from Axel's earlier rampage, it goes down hard and fast. Right on top of the man.

Skia and I are gone before he manages to scramble to his feet.

I leap through the open door to Agatha's backseat, nearly colliding with Kate, and Ags peels out of the alley.

Six

The route to Kate's Nona's house is fraught with tension. Partially because all three of the humans keep glancing back to check if Axel is tailing us—we have no idea what he drives, but I can only assume it's a very loud motorcycle. Partially because Skia has taken on a sulky demeanor and refuses to tell me why—even only in my head. And partially because Missy—as intelligent as she is after everything we've been through—has not ceased her efforts to capture and, I assume, eat the lizard.

Leaving the city doesn't take too long despite the usual Saturday afternoon traffic. We hit the plains, and Agatha follows Kate's directions down various backroads until the sun is low. The sepia-toned skyline seems flat despite the mountain range not far to the west.

Kate instructs Agatha to turn, and I swallow audibly.

"Uh, is this the place?"

Skia glides up from where they were resting on the floor of the car. They nestle into my lap, no longer in danger of the sun.

Hmm. Spooky.

I nod as Kate chuckles.

"Yeah. This is the family ranch. It used to be operational, but my dad left when he joined the army, and the rest of the aunts and uncles didn't have an interest in running things. So, it's just Nona now."

We pass under a large arched sign with missing letters. I'm unsure what it once said, but at present it reads *Cail--ach Ranc-.*

Ivy crawls up the wrought iron. Spiderwebs shimmer in the dim evening light. The gravel road leads through what appears to be waist-high fields of golden grass. Ahead, a three-story ranch house sits not far from an almost-as-large fading red barn. The only height around us comes from the buildings and a few scraggly trees surrounding them.

The lack of mountains, forests, anything on the horizon sends a shiver down my spine.

"This place has a... peculiar feel to it," Agatha murmurs. She drives slowly, taking us up to the house.

There is strong magic here.

Kate glances into the backseat with alarm in her gaze. She meets Skia's eye and quickly turns back around.

Missy darts to my side, probably sensing my anxiety. I run my fingers through her fur, and her warmth calms me.

The car slows to a stop. Only one downstairs window of the house is lit. The rest are black, gaping holes of darkness that, when combined with the peeling paint and dripping gutters, seem as though they want to swallow us whole.

I pull my sweatshirt back on, grateful to have it as I creak open the door and step into chilly evening air. The city holds a different kind of heat and, though I'm certain temperatures were high during the day, the disappearance of the sun leaves an unseasonable cold in the air.

Or maybe I'm shivering because I'm freaked out.

"How is this place," I mutter just for Skia's ears, "creepier than a coven of witches opening a pit to hell?"

They let out a light hissing laugh and reply, *Because you watch too many horror movies.*

Agatha gracefully steps out from the driver's seat, her multitude of skirts flowing behind her as the wind catches her hair.

"How do you look good after driving for two hours?" I grumble. I rub my face, dragging lines of sleep from my features as Skia takes their place at my shoulder.

Agatha lets out a soft chuckle. She looks around, eyes wide as she takes in the homestead-style house and barn. There are a multitude of garden beds between both. Raised boxes overflow with greenery. Chicken-wire surrounds many of them, a barricade to keep whatever animals that live out here from stealing vegetables.

Ags gives her skirts a flourish and runs a hand through her hair. "Magic."

I roll my eyes, hearing the joke in her voice even as I push away a taste of bitterness.

"Wait, Missy!" Ags calls as the little black cat scampers past.

"It's okay," I say with humor in my voice.

Missy leaps, bounding through the tall grass like a dancer. Her little yowls are happy ones and, after a minute of sprinting and spinning halfway across the field and back, she returns to my side and rubs against my shin.

I kneel on one knee. "Nice change of pace?"

Those yellow eyes fix on me. She flicks her tail across my hand.

"After this, I'll make a point of taking you to the park more."

Missy meows.

I'll be sure to remind them, Skia promises.

With a darted glance at the demon on my shoulder, my cat rubs her head across my hand. I give the ear scratches she's asking for and then rise to my feet.

Kate stands a few paces closer to the house, clutching the shoebox in her hands and looking back at us expectantly.

"Right, coming," I say.

"Do we want to hide the car or anything?" Agatha asks. "In case Axel catches up?"

I glance at the junker and then at the long drive we came up. "I think if he gets here, it's because he knows where we are. Feels like hiding the car won't do much."

Ags nods, clicks the lock on her key fob, and follows me toward the house.

We make it up the rickety steps of the wrap-around porch. A wide swing sits to the left, looking as though it has had better days and squeaking as a gentle breeze causes it to sway.

"Not getting less creepy," I murmur to Skia on my shoulder.

The demon hisses a laugh again.

Kate crooks an eyebrow up at me. She shifts the shoebox under one arm and reaches up to knock on the white, peeling door.

Before her knuckles find the wood, a shadow moves across the glass pane square, the handle turns, and the door swings open.

Nona is old. Old beyond what I'd expected from a grandmother of a twenty-something-year-old.

Her hunched figure screams crone with her gnarled knuckle bones protruding at odd angles and the liver spots that are barely visible against the multitude of freckles and wrinkles coating her skin. Her hair is white, each strand thick and coarse. She wears it long, braided nearly to her waist and decorated with wooden beads and dried-out flowers.

Her stern expression breaks into a grin the second Kate's face is illuminated by the foyer light.

With ushering hands and a gravelly voice, she pulls us all into the house.

"Nona." Kate deposits the shoebox onto a long end table and clutches her grandmother, burying her face in the woman's neck. She's nearly bent in half to collect the comfort from the much shorter woman.

"Katelyn," Nona says, patting her back. "My dear girl."

I swallow down a lump in my throat. Beside me, Agatha reaches out. Her hand closes around mine, and she gives me a squeeze. Missy presses against my legs. A whisp of Skia's shadowy form caresses my neck.

Their presence lightens some of the weight settled against my chest.

I grew up in a place similar to this. Open fields, wide farmlands. Small towns and small minds. I had one ally growing up. My grandmother.

Her passing was what sparked me to get out of that place.

I blink away the tears burning in my eyes and try to focus on the décor. A set of stairs to the right is walled with family pictures. More dried plants in vases and hanging from just about every place a hook would fit. And, as I carefully look everywhere but at the hug, I note things that I'd have missed a year ago.

There are scratches on the baseboards. Vaguely familiar symbols. I glance up and, sure enough, there are similar designs carved into the doorframe and the window ledges.

"Tell me, Kate," Nona's gravely voice grabs my attention. The woman gives us a cursory look; her eyes linger on Skia with a suspicious lack of surprise or fear. She turns to the box in Kate's hands. "What did the poor man do to deserve scales?"

Seven

Kate tells the story. From the infidelity to the purchasing of goods at Agatha's Emporium. When Nona raises an eyebrow, she sheepishly admits to her friend "borrowing" a "witchy-looking" book from Nona's library the last time they came for a visit.

To my surprise, the old woman doesn't look angry in the slightest. Instead, she cackles and tells Kate she's always liked that friend of hers.

We sit around a wooden kitchen table. Herbs dangle from every inch of wall space, much of which is taken up by warped wooden shelves stacked with everything from cookbooks to unnamed tomes that look as old as the one Kate showed us, glass jars with an assortment of odd things in them—and some more recognizable like salt, pepper, and cinnamon. The kitchen also includes a wall of hanging pots and pans, as well as one of those magnetic knife holders with a row of sharp instruments.

In the center of the table, a little gray shoebox holds the green and white lizard.

Introductions are made. Nona's lack of curiosity at Skia is explained when she politely asks them which brand of demon they are.

I hear the surprise in their voice as they whisper the answer across our minds. I'm certain we both share a curiosity about how this woman knows so much, but the question is cut off before it begins when Nona looks at Agatha and raises an eyebrow.

"I'm wondering why you lot came all this way when you could have handled this yourself."

"Oh." Ags glances at me, her dark eyes wide. "Well, I'm actually pretty new to this. I've done wiccan ceremonies for years, but actual magic is—"

"New to this plane, yes. I know dear. But it sounds like you're well read, and you had the book." She puts a hand on the top of the leather bound tome. "I'm glad you've all brought it back, but it does surprise me."

There was more than one reason for coming here, Skia says. They sit on the table in front of me, enjoying a plate of gingersnap cookies while Missy looks on from Ags's lap with a jealous gaze. *But this feels more like witch magic than the wiccan craft.*

Ags nods.

Nona scoffs. "What on earth are you talking about, my little demon friend?"

I clear my throat. "We ran across a coven of witches on the east coast not too long ago. I think it's the similarity of aggressive magic that feels like this isn't wiccan in nature."

"*Wiccan in nature*?" Nona's tone is heavy with incredulity. She throws a hand in the air, shaking her head and directing a glare at Ags and then Skia. "What nonsense."

"As we said," I mutter with growing annoyance. "We're brand new to all of this. Even Skia had been gone from this plane for over five-hundred years before they showed up in Missy."

"Yes." Nona turns her glare on me. "Showed up and reawakened a magic in the world that has been dormant for centuries."

Kate gulps.

Agatha shifts uncomfortably in her chair.

I glare back at the old woman.

Nona sighs. "It's not your fault," she placates, patting Ags's arm. "It sounds as though the two of you," she glances from Ags to Skia, "are of the belief that wiccan and witch mean two different things."

"Don't they?" I ask, my brow furrowed.

The shoebox at the center of the table wiggles. Missy's gaze shifts from the cookies to it, her eyes narrowed.

"Not in the slightest."

Agatha frowns. "I was always told wiccans work for the common good while witches aim for power, usually from demonic sources. The witches in Salem certainly seemed as though they felt the same."

"Young ones," Nona grumbles. "I'm plenty powerful without help from those bums in hell, thank you very much."

Her tone replaces my defensive frustration with a snort.

She grins at me. "Looks like we need a refill on cookies. And I could certainly use some tea if I'm going to spend my evening educating the lot of you and reversing my granddaughter's ill-advised revenge spell."

Across the table, Kate flushes. She mumbles, "Sorry Nona."

"Oh, it's fine Katelyn. Now, put some water on to boil while I find the rest of the gingersnaps. Then the lesson begins."

"There is no true difference between wiccan magic and witchcraft. The terminology began to change when people who focused on healing and defensive magic were called wiccan by the populace. Those of us more geared toward offensive spells were deemed witches. There was plenty of cross-casting, but of course, as with all things, rumors spread and politics came into it. After a few centuries, witches were painted in a much darker color than our wiccan counterparts. Though, as I said before, there is no true difference between the two."

Agatha stares open-mouthed at Nona. Awkward uncertainty clouds her expression as she swallows and begins an apology.

The grandmother—the witch—waves it away and takes a sip of her jasmine tea. "Worry over it no longer, darling. How could you possibly know? Rumors and gossip become truth when there is no one to teach real history."

I chuckle. "Who taught you the real history?"

"Took the question right outta my mouth," Kate says with a smirk. "And why didn't I know about any of this, Nona?"

Nona turns a glare on her granddaughter again. "Don't start with that. I've invited you over time and again to learn my old secrets, and you've rejected every offer."

Kate doesn't flinch away from the tone, instead she rolls her eyes. "Well, I thought you were talking about farming secrets!"

Skia's haunting laugh fills the heads of everyone in the kitchen, and the rest of us join them in a round of chuckles.

Nona stands with a groan and pats Agatha's shoulder. "Don't worry yourself about it. I'm happy to share what I know with the new generation. Now." She surveys us as she fills her teacup again. "What is the other reason you came here?"

The last of my laughter dies in my throat. My expression sours as I recall the predatory look Axel trained on Skia back at Agatha's Emporium. Nona turns to me.

"Ohh," she murmurs. "Something serious then." She gestures a liver-spotted hand at the box on the table. "More serious than questionable spell-work."

Kate has the gall to look offended before she gives a half-hearted shrug and picks up a cookie.

"Our incident back east seems to have put us on the radar of a bounty hunter," Agatha says softly. "He's after Skia, though it seems he's also stealing anything magical he can find along the way."

Nona looks at Skia. "Who hired him?"

My lip curls. "Hell. According to what he said the first time he found us." I wave a hand agitatedly through the air. "There was a whole monologue."

"They do enjoy those," Nona says, her gaze still thoughtfully fixed on Skia. "And you don't want to go back?"

I move my hands, reaching across the table to curl my arms around my friend. "No, they don't."

I'd rather not descend to the plane of fire and suffering again. No.

"And you all." Nona looks to the rest of us, taking her time to meet every eye. "You have no issue keeping a demon in your midst? You do not agree that this creature should be returned to damnation?"

Silence permeates the kitchen. My heartbeat thunders in my chest, a renewed worry for my friend seeping into my chest.

My jaw is tight as I stand from the table. The chair scrapes across the ground. "Skia has every right to exist," I murmur. "They have a right to be safe and happy and cared for."

Demi.

The whisper of the word, in all our heads evidenced by the softening of Nona's expression.

Agatha nods.

Kate gives an audible gulp and then pipes up, "I haven't known Skia long, but they seem nice. And they didn't judge me for turning Trevor into a lizard so..."

I wouldn't dare to judge you for the act. Even the spell itself was quite impressive, especially for one brand new to witchy magic.

"Brand new to magic," Agatha corrected softly. She frowned at the grandmother, who had picked up a bell jar and was sprinkling herbs into it. "Does this mean I can do more? More than the protection symbols and wards and things?"

"Oh," Nona says with a grin. She turns, her face catching the light and giving her wrinkly skin an eerie glow. "Much more, deary. And I can help teach—"

Her offer is cut off by a sound that sends a shiver down my spine and causes my lower back to start sweating.

The distant roar of a motorcycle coming up the gravel path.

Eight

Now is a good time to show our new friend the protection magic you've been practicing.

Skia darts across the table, hops over Kate's shoulder, and swishes up to look out the window above the sink. Plants cover the ledge, and Skia could almost be mistaken for a shadow amongst the multitude of dark leaves.

I move with them, leaning in toward the glass in time to catch sight of a headlight before it disappears behind the car. A second later, my guess that it's Axel is confirmed via the outline of the man against the moonlight as he strides toward the house.

Agatha sets Missy on the table and glances at Nona. "With your permission?"

Nona smiles, the curve of her lips bringing her laugh lines into stark contrast. "This man has been following you for some time?"

I turn from the window and nod. "Seems like he's been looking for us for months."

The old woman sets down the bell jar. She pats Agatha's arm with a very grandmotherly smile. "Why don't you let me help with this one, dear? It's been a long while since I've had the opportunity to stretch my magic."

Missy yowls. Standing on the table, she paws the lizard box once before jumping down. With a flick of her yellow eyes in my direction, she gestures with a paw and follows Nona and Agatha toward the front door.

Kate scoops the shoebox from the table, opens a cupboard, and tucks it inside. She glances at me. "Are you bringing anything to this fight with a bounty hunter from hell?"

I can't help but chuckle at her dry tone. Part of me takes offense to the question, but I push that part down. It's obvious she didn't mean anything by it. And it's a fair ask.

Still, magic or not, I *need* a way to help my friends. So, I grab one of the knives on the magnet block and gesture for her to lead the way.

Kate grins. "This is nuts." She takes a blade as well and hurries after the others.

Demi. Skia floats along the counter toward me, stopping a few inches from the point of the knife. *I think you should stay in here.*

I snort. "No chance." Then I puff out a sigh. Even with a powerful—though how powerful is yet to be discovered—witch on our side, the thought of going up against Axel is terrifying.

Because if he gets through us, who knows who he'll go after next?

Fine, Skia hisses. *But please try to be careful.*

"Aww, are you worried?" I ask in a teasing tone. Skia glowers and hops onto my shoulder.

With the kitchen knife clenched tight in my hand, I walk us both into the foyer.

I meet the others at the front door just as a heavy thud slams against the wood.

"Keep that up," Nona says to Agatha.

My friend has pulled her dark hair into a ponytail and has both hands out, pouring defensive magic into the doorway.

Kate takes the stairs, standing a few steps up with her blade at the ready. Agatha and Nona face the door head-on, and I'm to the right, my breath shallow as what I can only assume is Axel's body or boot hits the door again.

Missy waits under the table beside the stairs. She glances at me for a brief moment before turning her attention back to the door. Her tail swishes silently back and forth.

"One more should do it." Nona raises a walking cane in her left hand, the right fingers twisted and tight as blue electric light sparks across her skin.

My eyes widen. A chest-tightening reminder of the witches who tried to kill me and force Skia back to hell briefly engulfs my focus. I swallow down the memory. Kate, standing across from me on the stairs, looks as awed and frightened as I feel. She stares at her grandmother like she's never seen the woman before.

The *one more* comes swift and hard. The warped air around the door fractures and dissolves as Agatha lowers her hands.

"You okay?" I shoot her a glance.

She nods, sweat on her brow. "He's strong."

Nona cackles. "Good."

The door splinters and crashes open. Wood flies across the room, shards hitting everyone except Ags, who manages to pop up her shield bubble just in time.

Standing in the doorway, the hulking figure of a hellish Australian bounty hunter blocks the moonlight.

"Well, well, well," Axel says. I assume he looks at each of us, though it's impossible to tell through the thick aviator sunglasses. "Looks like I'm raking in quite the payday."

Kate scowls. "Yeah, I don't think so, dude."

He sneers, turning his head toward the stairs. "You reek of untamed magic. Which means you've cast a spell recently. Hell will pay a lot to find out how you came into witchcraft."

"Hmm." Nona shifts, the cane in her hand directed at the man even as a curious expression flitters across her face. "Why?" She jerks her head in my direction. "I understand the desire to bring back one of their own. It doesn't look good for a shadow demon to be running free when the more powerful forces are still locked away. But why go after spellcasters? Why collect magic items?"

My palms are damp with sweat. The kitchen knife is worn from use, finger grooves not quite fitting to my larger hand.

Axel shrugs. "I don't ask questions when this much gold is on the line."

"Gold?" Agatha raises an eyebrow. Her hands tremble, from the exertion of the protection on the door or fear.

At this, the bounty hunter gestures toward the ground with the weapon in his hand. "They haven't updated to direct deposit down there."

Kate snorts.

"I'm afraid you won't be receiving a payday," Nona says. "Not after attacking these kind children and threatening my granddaughter."

She raises the cane. A blast of light shoots through the room, white-hot and electric. Skia slips down my back, clinging to my waist as they hide from the brightness.

I bring up my hand to protect my eyes, but before I've gotten halfway, the light is gone.

A laugh cuts through the air. I swallow, heart pounding as fear cuts in again.

Axel stands in front of the door. Lightly smoking, but otherwise uninjured. He laughs harder, pointing his blade at Nona. "That would have hurt, witch. I'm not a betting man, but I'd put money down on hell payin' more for you than the rest of them put together."

Kate lets out a furious curse, and Agatha steps in front of Nona with her hands raised in a defensive gesture I've seen before.

But my attention is not caught on his words. I frown, head tilted as the bits of smoke coming off his leather jacket seem to follow an invisible trail to the silver charm hooked at his belt.

It glows, ever so faintly. I grit my teeth with realization.

"Impressive protection," Nona murmurs. She doesn't look or sound as confident as she had a moment ago. "A gift from your employers?"

Axel grins. "Something like that. Now, I don't have room for all of you on my bike. But the demon will fit in a cage, and the heart of a witch is worth almost as much as the whole."

He tosses me a secondary glance. "I don't suppose you have a human bounty anywhere? Or are you a complete waste of my time?"

Heat rushes to my cheeks as a combination of embarrassment and fury slams through my veins. I open my mouth to respond.

A high-pitched yowl, amplified to ear-shattering volume by the vaulted ceiling, splits the air.

Missy launches out from under the table, aiming straight for Axel.

Nine

"Missy!" I lunge. Bone-deep worry for my cat overrides any sense of self-preservation.

The little black ball of fluffy feline fury moves quicker than I've ever seen. She swipes. Her claws go through the leather cord holding Axel's silver charm to his belt. The small ball thunks onto the hardwood floor.

Missy bats it across the room and darts to her spot under the table just as Axel's boot flies past where she'd just been.

I'm still moving. Not as quick as my cat, and definitely not as able to stop or turn on a dime.

The realization that Missy is out of immediate range of harm comes too late. I slam into Axel hard enough to knock him back. He hits the doorframe. Swings his arm.

A burst of pain erupts across my side, and a scream escapes my lips.

Jumbled sounds are just audible past my own heartbeat and heavy breathing.

Agatha shouts my name, high and shrill and more terrified than I've ever heard her before.

Skia hisses the same, rage erupting into all our heads as the little demon screeches bloody murder.

Footsteps pound on the stairs and Kate is at my side, helping lift me from the ground and backing us both away from Axel's blade. The shiny silver is coated in my blood.

The final sound is familiar. Sharp crackling, like a brush fire or dry air right before a thunderstorm.

My vision is blurred, but I make out the fear plastered across Axel's face. He lost his sunglasses while stabbing me.

He meets my gaze for a split second, mouth open as though he's going to try another threat or beg for his life.

He doesn't have time to utter a sound.

I shield my eyes again, and lightning slams into his chest.

With no protection, the scent of burning leather, then flesh, quickly engulfs the room. I look at Nona, hunched over with effort as she goes Emperor Palpatine on the Australian bounty hunter. Her face is red, hair almost glowing with the same blue/white light. But the light begins to fade. The electricity sputters, the line thinning though Axel is still standing.

Agatha is transfixed by the ancient powerful figure Nona is in this moment. My friend glances at me, clenches her jaw, and puts a hand on Nona's arm.

At once, the power amplifies. I have to close my eyes; the light is too bright. I feel a warmth on my chest and recognize Missy's claws as she gently kneads them into my shirt.

And then it's done.

The sound ends. My eyelids no longer glow with the brilliance of the lightning.

I open them slowly, half terrified of what I will see. But where I'd expect a charred corpse is simply a pile of ash and melted metal. The wire frames from Axel's aviators are a few feet away. One of the shades is missing.

"Is..." Agatha's voice is hoarse, as though she's been screaming. "Is everyone okay?"

Kate replies, her voice higher than usual, "Demi needs help."

"Nah, I'm—" I'm about to say fine when a set of kitty toe-beans plant onto my lips. Missy glares at me from her spot on my chest.

Just below her, my shirt is torn and a bloody gash oozes like a babbling brook, staining the wood of the stairs a lovely maroon color.

It occurs to me, as the thought floats across the front of my mind, that blood loss might be affecting my cognition.

Demi. Skia is at my side in a flash. They curl around the railing of the stairs, eyes narrowed on my wound and then on my hazel eyes. *What were you thinking?*

I open my mouth.

Never mind, Skia growls. *I know. Missy was in danger. Agatha!*

She's with us before he finishes saying her name, crouched in front of me—there is no room on the stairs with my sprawling limbs and Kate still behind me cradling my head.

Huh. I try to lift it. I manage to get free of her hands, but the effort makes me dizzy. I lean back again.

"Dammit," Agatha mutters. "Demi, hold still okay? I'm going to try something."

"Maybe some gauze or something?" I ask, my voice slurred.

She shakes her head and plants her hands on my side. I want to protest. She's getting blood all over her lace sleeves.

But my voice isn't working. My mouth isn't moving properly. The blur moves in, the faces of my family fading as the pain in my side also fades.

I swallow. I wanted to say something. Wanted my final words to be a bit more substantial than "some gauze or something." But I've lost my chance.

It's not fear that grips me now. Now that the pain has turned to numbness, I have room for other sensations. Overwhelming warmth fills my chest. I never expected to die this young, but I also never expected to do it surrounded by people who care for me. Who love me.

I feel the smile on my lips, the pressure of Missy on my chest, and the coal-like heat of Skia, their little tendrils twisted around my hand.

And then I don't feel anything.

Ten

Waking up is something like a slow-motion rewind of an old VHS tape. Scenes play out across my eyelids. Axel barging through the door. His charm fending off Nona's power. Missy's daring leap to destroy his protection. My foolish move to try and keep my cat safe.

The knife.

The blood.

I open my eyes, and my vision returns the same way it went, everything fading back into existence.

Agatha kneels on the ground before me. Her hands, sleeves, and skirts are soaked with blood. She's still pressing her hands to my side. Pale fingers are latched around her wrists, and I turn my head just enough to spot Kate looking absolutely exhausted on the step behind me.

"What happened?" I mumble. My mouth is so dry it hurts to talk.

Ags looks up, and my eyes widen at the tear tracks running down her cheeks. "Demi," she breathes.

Missy yowls, rubbing her head across my chin and licking my cheek with her sand-papery tongue.

Skia lets out a hitched sob of relief in my head.

Behind Ags, Nona looks on with a tired gaze. "That was impressive work, Agatha."

My friend moves her hands from my side. The gash across my skin is entirely scabbed over. The sight of it brings back some pain, but nothing like the searing agony that was present a few moments ago.

"Couldn't have done it without Kate," Ags says, giving the woman behind me a grateful nod.

I attempt to sit straight, but everything sways before me. Hands go up to stop me from moving.

"Fine," I say, my mouth still not quite working. "But would someone tell me what happened?"

Skia bobs a bit on the stair railing. *And maybe we can get them some water?*

I nod, a poor choice as everything continues bobbing up and down long after my head stops moving.

"Agreed," Nona says softly. "Perhaps we retire to the living room, let Demi lay down for a bit, and refill everyone with some food."

"Sounds great," I groan. "How am I getting there?"

Two days later, we are all still at Nona's ranch. Kate called her roommate to reassure her that she wasn't a missing person, and

Agatha did the same with her landlord, blaming the mess on vandals and promising to pay for the windows as soon as she returns.

My apartment was locked when we left so my only concerns are my leftovers going bad and my plants needing a good soak when we get back.

Nona's front door is fixed. Agatha has been poring over spell books since the morning after my near-death experience. It didn't take her long to find one to mend simple things, though it did take a few tries to get the entire door back into place without any missing pieces.

I plop another mini-cinnamon roll into my mouth and follow it up with a sip from my nearly black coffee. The little shoebox on the table before me jiggles.

Missy bats at it with a paw but stops when I offer her a strip of bacon.

I would like more of the fried pig as well, Skia hisses from their place beside me.

At the stove, Kate chuckles and uses a pair of tongs to set three more strips on Skia's plate.

"You're sure you have to leave?" Nona asks, her gaze lovingly fixed on her granddaughter.

Kate nods. "School is starting soon. I need to go talk to my counselor and re-adjust my schedule."

I grin.

We both plan on leaving gaps in our classes so there is time to drive out here every other week or so. Kate and Agatha both have a lot to learn in the magic department and, while I don't have the innate magic they do, I plan on at least reading up on the history of all this stuff.

Nona turns her gaze on me, and her expression grows serious. "Demi, come with me a moment, would you? We have something to discuss."

She inclines her head at Missy, who nods and darts from the table after her.

I glance at Skia, who does their bouncy shrug, and then stand with a groan and follow the woman into the living room. The couch cushions are a little stained with my blood, but it's difficult to see unless you're looking for it. The maroon and gold patterned fabric is a good disguise.

"My dear," she says, turning to face me as Missy jumps onto the coffee table before the fireplace. "You already know you don't have any latent magical ability."

My face flushes. I nod, biting away the disappointment that comes with her words.

"However, you do have this cat."

Missy's yellow gaze surveys Nona. I almost imagine she raises a kitty eyebrow.

"Missy is really smart," I say, unsure where this is going.

"Well, she's more than that, actually. She has all the makings of a familiar. And, while it will take a lot more work from you than your friends, with her help, you may be able to learn how to practice magic."

My jaw goes slack. I glance at Missy and find her staring at me with a similar stunned expression. Sort of like the time I dropped her tuna treats down the sink on accident.

"She could..." I stumble over the words, looking from Missy to my own hands with excitement trembling in my veins. "We could do magic together?"

Nona shrugs. "It's very possible. This is the most intelligent animal I've ever come across. And she has a connection to the mystical elements of the world. It will take work, mind you." Her eyes narrow into a very school-teacher expression. "Lots of work."

"I don't mind work," I murmur. My skin buzzes with anticipation. I want to start now, to pull down a spell book and train immediately. But logic overrides the idea of staying here another week to get started.

We have time. Lots of time. And Agatha knows a few people who might have some of that latent magic Nona was telling us about. We plan on bringing them next time.

"Now." Nona pats my arm and winks. "We'd better go de-lizard that young man before he develops a permanent taste for grasshoppers."

I snort. The old woman returns to the kitchen, and I crouch with a wince to get even with Missy's eyeline.

"Hey pretty girl." I reach behind her ears and give the scratches she loves so much. "Who knew you'd be so powerful, huh?"

Her nose twitches. She licks me.

Nona waits until the car is packed (she's sending us with copious amounts of gingersnap cookies and magical texts) before she undoes Kate's spell on Trevor.

It takes a surprisingly short amount of time. She mutters a few words, throws a grayish concoction on his lizard body, and then the scales melt away. The lizard is replaced by a tall man with a mop of brown hair and a tank-top tan.

The tan is visible because the poor guy returned to human form without the blessing of clothes.

Kate chucks a spare pair of shorts and a T-shirt at him while the rest of us avert our gazes. Then, Nona steps forward for a few words.

"It's been a rough few days for you. And I'm sorry it took us so long to get you back to two legs. We were all a bit drained for a while there. Now, I know my Kate didn't behave in the most mature way, but I want you to hear me right now."

She moves closer, her finger pressing into the buttons of his borrowed shirt. "You remember those little grasshoppers you ate as a lizard? The crunch of the exoskeleton and the papery texture of the wings? If you do or say anything to put my granddaughter in jeopardy, you will not have the luxury of being turned into a lizard. You will be a bug."

Her tone is kind and old womanly, but her words cause Trevor to blanch.

He nods fervently, glances at the lot of us, then follows Kate's pointed finger to the car waiting out front.

It's a tense drive home. We drop Trevor off at his frat house. Agatha follows him to the porch steps, giving another warning for him to keep his mouth shut—and probably reminding him why he was turned into a lizard to begin with—before letting him go inside.

We stop by the Emporium. I can feel Agatha's sadness at the state of her store, but she puts on a smile and shakes her head.

"It's fine." She wiggles her many ringed fingers. "I know how to use magic to fix things."

It doesn't look like much was stolen, but she and Kate work together to at least patch up the glass windows so we can lock the place.

"That will do for now." Agatha heaves a sigh and wipes her brow. Then she looks at me. "Chinese? Your place?"

I grin and turn at Kate. "Wanna join? We know a place with the best egg rolls."

Our new friend smiles but shakes her head. "I really should check in with my roommates. At this point, they probably don't believe my texts. I don't want them calling the cops about a missing person."

"Fair enough," I say with a chuckle.

"But I'll give you guys a call tomorrow?" Kate glances between the two of us with slight apprehension. "I'd love to come help fix up the Emporium."

Agatha nods. "We'd love that too."

It's a quiet rest of the evening. The food is delicious. Skia talks me into ordering an extra side of dumplings, and they practically inhale them all before letting them cool. The steam rising up from their shadowy form makes me burst out laughing.

I clutch my side as my scab flares with pain. But it fades quickly. We settle onto the couch, Missy on my lap, eating canned tuna from a pretty porcelain bowl. Skia is in the planters above us, their shadowy tendrils reaching down every now and then to grab an additional spring roll.

Agatha sits beside me, ignoring the Psych rerun and the food in favor of the book she borrowed from Nona. "This is fascinating," she murmurs, her dark eyes scanning the pages with awe.

I dig through my take-out box with my chopsticks, searching for the last piece of broccoli. "It was kind of Nona to share them with us."

She nods, pulled from the book as her gaze meets mine. "It's kind of her to train us, and to open her home to anyone else who wants to learn."

"You're starting something amazing," I say to her, my heart warming with the words.

Agatha shakes her head and reaches over to scratch behind Missy's ears. The cat looks up briefly before deciding scratches aren't interrupting her meal and continues eating.

"Technically," Agatha chuckles, "this one started something amazing."

"*You all did,*" Skia hisses.

"We," I correct immediately. "*We* all did."

"We sure did," Ags says with a smile. "And I can't wait to see where it goes from here."

Acknowledgements

This book is for everyone who poured so much love into Spooky Cat. You've all inspired this beautiful version (thanks, Tracey, for doing the cover).

Spooky Cat started as a lark. A fun story to write with zero consequences or expectation. Now the gang lives rent-free in my head, their adventures calling me to put them on paper so others can join in the fun.

Thank you for believing in Demi, Skia, Missy, and Ags. Without you, they would have been a one-hit wonder.

About the author

C.H. Lyn lives in Colorado with her husband and two far-too-intelligent little girls. The family travels often, both for adventure and for her husband's military career. Lyn is an avid grower of the community, believing that what you put into the world is what you get out of it. She has a plethora of works, all of which can be found at chlyn.com.

www.ingramcontent.com/pod-product-compliance
Lightning Source LLC
Chambersburg PA
CBHW030335310726
48979CB00001B/33
9781960659248